I Hear My

Lighthouse

Calling

A PORT JAMES SERIES

Written and Illustrated by

JAY DIEDRECK

ISBN 978-1-63903-662-2 (paperback)
ISBN 978-1-63903-663-9 (digital)

Christian Faith Publishing, Inc.
832 Park Avenue
Meadville, PA 16335
www.christianfaithpublishing.com

This book is a work of fiction. Names, characters, places, and incidents are the product of the author's imagination or are used fictitiously. Any resemblance to actual events, locales, or persons, living or dead, is coincidental.

Printed in the United States of America

Dedicated to my love and joy, Alicia

Special thanks to,
JMB and CAD

Contents

CHAPTER 1

Wakening in Port James

2019

It was morning in Port James when Abby opened the screen door from her parents' home. Raising their family here, the Watercrests had lived in this little home for more than fifty years. Abby quietly stepped onto the sunny front porch. She reclined her frame into one of the two wooden Adirondack chairs, being careful not to spill her coffee. Since Abby had just finished her four-year business degree from the local college, it was now time to relax. Over the past three weeks, she learned the enjoyment of sights and sounds around her as much as the quiet time to think about things.

Looking across the village street from her vantage point, she said to herself, "I think I made my coffee and got out here quietly enough not to wake Mom and Dad. However, I'm sure one of them…probably Dad, will join me soon."

Abby pulled her long-sleeve fisherman's knit sweater halfway up her arms. Over the last few weeks, the early summer sun had kissed her arms and face, making her freckles delightfully apparent. Mornings along coastal Maine were still chilly but would eventually give up to warmer breezes, something Abby was looking forward to. Warmer weather also seemed to agree with her son.

"Maybe today I will accompany Dad on his way along the footpath to the Port James lighthouse."

Being the lighthouse keeper of Port James light, her dad, she knew, would soon have to start his duties to keep the structure and accompanied gift shop in good condition.

With Abby's pleasant routine of greeting the morning, she learned to distinguish familiar and reassuring sounds flowing like an innocent song from her little village. Just across the street and down a ways, she heard a familiar, light squeaking sound. It came from the red and white canvas awning on Walker's grocery as it was unfurled. Abby could envision that Adam Walker was reaching upward with his metal pole to secure a ratchet on the side of his building. With a twisting motion, he was opening the awning for a new business day. His next task would be using a natural straw broom to sweep and freshen the sidewalk.

As her vision disappeared, she looked up just in time to see twelve-year-old Dale delivering the morning newspaper on his bicycle. While carefully coasting past each home, he reached into his bike's wire basket. With each toss, a folded newspaper landed next to the owner's mailbox with a light thump.

From the maple trees overhead, Abby heard robins and sparrows singing through the air in hopes of attracting a suitable mate for another season. A few other birds were already enjoying some splashing in the front yard birdbath. This morning, three sparrows were on the rim waiting for a robin in the center of the shallow bowl to finish.

Abby gazed down with a smile at the white cream in her cup, which was making an artistic little spiral. She took the cup up to her lips and, after inhaling a little of the aroma, enjoyed a sip of her pumpkin spice coffee. Like on cue, Abby heard her dad's footsteps as he descended the gray-painted wooden stairs to the foyer.

Klem paused a moment while reaching down to greet his tiger cat named Rose. He stood back up and looked for Abby through the screen door. Rose was still massaging his pant leg with the side of her whiskered cheek. With a gentle push on the door, he announced, "Good morning, my four-year English major graduate and my pretty blue-eyed daughter of Port James! May I join you this fine morning that God made for us? How did you sleep last night?"

Abby smiled and then placed her coffee on the wicker side table and eased out of her porch chair to give Klem a hug.

"Good morning back to you, Dad! Yes, I did have a good sleep, and you also look well rested. Hey, I wanted to tell you something. Yesterday, while you were at the lighthouse, I took Parker to watch Lloyd work on the village storage shed behind their offices. You know, the one next to the fireman's field. That little son of mine was so cute! He followed Lloyd around like a little duck. During this last visit, he became so mesmerized while watching Lloyd hammer the hand-split cedar shakes on that shed roof."

In thought, Klem looked down at his work shoes, rubbed his sideburn a little, and then said, "Why yes, Parker sure has taken a fondness to that man-friend of yours. I can also see that Lloyd likes Parker quite a bit."

Abby took another sip of her drink, pulled her long black hair around to the back of her neck, and answered, "It seems that when Parker is with Lloyd, he hardly seems to have any ailments at all. It is really beautiful!"

* * * * *

Parker came into Abby's life very unexpectedly. His birth mother had left the Port James area, abandoning her innocent and sweet six-year-old son in the care of social services. Her boyfriend left her as soon as she became pregnant, unfortunately a common occurrence. Before leaving for places unknown, she had him sign all the legal papers removing him and her from all parental status.

Within days, the little boy became a foster child with the Watercrests. It was the sincere hope of the social worker that they would someday fully adopt the child. With all the instability in his young life, Parker latched onto Abby and, within months, started to call her *mom*. Shortly afterward, he also called Klem and Jane his grandparents. It did not take long at all for Parker to love this new family of his. Of course, they totally loved and adored him as well.

There were many late-night discussions around the Watercrest's kitchen table as to Parker's future. They all agreed that as soon as social service could get the paperwork together, Abby would officially adopt little Parker.

Feeling Pretty Good

This morning's next appearance was Jane, Klem's wife of forty-nine years. She looked through the front window giving her a view of the porch's left side. Parker was tagging along behind her a little but holding tightly to his grandma's hand.

"Hey, you two out there! So do you want breakfast on the porch or in the back sunroom?"

Six-year-old Parker looked up at Jane and said with a little, quiet voice, "Can we have pancakes in the sunroom with the windows open? Today is washday, and I love to smell the fresh laundry and the sea breeze when we are eating."

Jane replied, "Sure, Parker, we can have breakfast out there, but I haven't started the laundry yet. All right, my handsome husband, who needs a haircut, and, Abby, let's start the migration to the sunroom. Is crispy bacon with breakfast going to work for everyone?"

It didn't take this little family much time at all to find their chairs around the round oak table in the sunroom. But before the first bite, Klem Watercrest asked for a moment for prayer. He looked around the table with his steel blue eyes, then folded his hands and bowed his head.

"This is the day that the Lord has made, let us rejoice and be glad in it!"

"Dear heavenly Father and Creator, thank You for keeping us safe throughout the night and making this morning for us to live."

At this time, Klem paused and opened one eye to look at Parker. He felt most thankful that this little boy, whom he called his grandson, had another day to live.

"We thank You for the love we share in our family. We ask that You bless us all with good health, and thank You for this fantastic breakfast. Amen."

Jane passed the blue serving plates around the table while each took their portion. Parker crossed his little thin legs behind his chair and happily started to wiggle his feet. Spearing his pancake with his fork, he looked at his "grandparents" and his "mom" and said, "Grandpa, I feel pretty good today! Maybe this will be a super fine day for me. Maybe I can climb the lighthouse all the way to the top…if I take it slowly."

Klem looked seriously at his grandson, then mustered a supporting smile.

"Well, big guy, maybe you will manage that, but I think your mom has another idea for you. While having coffee on the front porch this morning, your mom said…well, I will let her tell you what she has planned."

Parker took a chew of his bacon and looked across the table at his mom for an answer. Placing the blue linen napkin from her lap to the table, she said, "Lloyd gave me a call last night just before it became dark, around nine o'clock. See, he had finished the shed in the village and now has to take the scrap pieces of lumber and plywood away. Instead of throwing it all out in the construction dumpster that he rented, Lloyd was wondering if you wanted to make a tree fort with him today. He said that you could use the scrap lumber to make it."

Parker uncrossed his legs and, as he pushed his chair away, stood up straight and announced, "Yeah! One hundred and fourteen percent! Absolutely! I knew today would be great!"

With that expression of excitement, Parker took his last forkful of pancake and, with a swish of milk, raced upstairs to put on his sneakers. Klem thought about Parker's wonderful enthusiasm, and in many ways, it made him feel a little younger. He took off his wire-framed eyeglasses and started cleaning them with his napkin. Jane reached over and placed her hand on top of his and said in loving tones, "Honey, you know perfectly well that you have been wiping your handsomely shaped lips with that same linen napkin. With your attempt to clean your spectacles, instead, you are going to smear maple syrup all over them. Here, please take this clean one."

Of course, Klem decided that his lovely wife was right, so taking her donation, he exchanged the napkins. After finishing that task, he placed his glasses back on and looked at his daughter. With a concerned look, he asked, "Abby, I believe you took Parker to the doctor yesterday. We haven't had a chance to talk to you about what the Doc had to say. Did he have any more information about his recovery?"

Abby felt they could talk freely since Parker would be upstairs in his bedroom and out of earshot.

"Well...Dad and Mom, you know how thoroughly Dr. Randall explains things. He reviewed the symptoms of Parker's Lyme disease, which is fatigue, pain, weakness, muscle aches, and sometimes difficulty with thinking. As you know, we brought Parker to see Dr. Randall as soon as we removed that darn black-legged deer tick from below his skin.

"Unfortunately, the bull's-eye pattern was already apparent. All this because of that darn bacteria called bacterium *Borrelia burgdorferi*. The amoxicillin the doctor had us give Parker should have taken care of the symptoms. As we all have noticed, the bacteria and the symptoms are still bothering Parker. So now, Dr. Randall believes Parker has an autoimmune response; sometimes it is called...hmm... let me take out my notes."

Abby reached into her pocketbook, which was on the floor next to her chair, and found a white tablet of paper. Flipping through the pages, she found the information she wanted to share.

"I wrote down here that it is called posttreatment Lyme disease syndrome or PTLDS, also known as chronic Lyme disease."

Jane had a worried look in her usually bright and cheerful eyes. Waiting a moment to collect her thoughts, she asked, "Abby dear, if it is chronic, does that mean that Parker will never get better? I mean, he has his whole life in front of him, our poor grandson!"

Placing the notepaper back into her purse, Abby looked up the staircase to make sure Parker was still in his bedroom.

"Well, the doctor said that this could take several months, maybe even a whole year before he feels his old self again. As you know, Parker has good days and bad days with this darn bacterial infection from that tick. We have to make sure he eats nutritionally well and gets enough rest, even if it means taking a nap in the middle of the day. The good news is that Parker's body will probably get better. It will just take time."

Klem reached over to Jane and Abby, and together, Klem offered a prayer.

"Dear heavenly Father, thank You for life and good health. As Parker's body is working to combat these ailments, we ask that You give him Your almighty healing power. Please restore Parker's body to complete healing and health. We love this little grandson of ours, and thank You for his innocent life. We thank You for all good gifts You have blessed us with during our stay here on earth. In Jesus's precious name, we pray. Amen."

CHAPTER 3

Lloyd

Lloyd stepped up onto the Watercrest's porch, adjusted his leather carpenter's belt, and knocked on their hunter green screen doorframe. Cupping his hands around his mouth, he yelled, "Hey! Is anyone awake in there this morning?"

Without a wasted moment, Abby quickly excused herself from the breakfast table and skipped to the door to greet Lloyd. With the exchange of broad smiles, Abby went into Lloyd's innocent embrace. He felt Abby's arms eagerly reaching around his well-developed back, pulling him into her. Lloyd whispered a "Wow!" into her ear, and then they pulled back. With another assessment of her man-friend, Abby said, "Well, look at you, my handsome friend. You wear that carpenter's belt pretty nicely, looks like you might build something this fine morning."

At that moment, Parker came bouncing down the stairs, two at a time, and ran up to Lloyd to give him a squeeze. With his short stature, his head just reached Lloyd's chest. Without hesitation, Lloyd reached down and picked up Parker so they could be face-to-face.

"Hey, Parker, I bought you something that you might just be able to use today!"

He reached into the side loop of his carpenter's belt and, drawing it out, presented him with a ten-ounce hammer.

"Let's put your new hammer to good use today, Parker! I think we were fixing to construct a dollhouse for you to play with!"

Parker rolled his eyes while his lips made a smile from ear to ear. He enjoyed Lloyd's sense of humor and also understood it quite well. Turning to his grandparents and his mom, who was back at the table, he exclaimed, "We men are going to build a tree fort in the backyard! He said that there is plenty enough scrap wood left over from one of his construction sites. All we have to do is pick it up and load the perfectly fine wood in his truck. Mr. Lloyd said so, and look at this brand-new hammer he bought me! I can hardly wait to drive nails into some plywood! Boy, oh boy, let's go, Mr. Lloyd!"

By this time, everyone was exchanging smiles with each other, a perfect way to continue the morning. Abby pointed to her son and said, "Don't forget your work jacket, Parker. The air is still carrying a little chill. And, Lloyd, dear, make sure you both come back here in time for lunch at one o'clock. Dad is smoking some salmon outside on the grill. He is planning to use it for a pasta noodle casserole. So don't miss out. Okay?"

The two gave a wave in the air and took to the waiting truck in their driveway. Jane looked at her daughter and said, "My oh my, Abby! Lloyd certainly is nice to Parker. They seem to hit it off so well. I can hardly believe it has been two whole years ago when Parker lost his dad. The social worker explained in full detail that awful fishing boat accident. If I recall, she also said that after his dad's death, poor Parker stopped talking for over a month."

"Of course, Lloyd will never take the place of his father, but it sure is nice to see him happy once again. Abby, it also seems that your man-friend understands Parker's limitations with the Lyme disease."

In the truck, Lloyd helped Parker adjust his seat belt, and then they headed to where the scrap plywood and lumber was stacked at the shed construction site. It didn't take too long to arrive at the shed and the woodpile. Lloyd backed up his truck and engaged his parking brake, and the two piled out to relocate the wood to the bed of the truck. They were there for only about fifteen minutes when poor Parker's body started to wear down. With his hand on his little friend's shoulder, Lloyd said, "Well, Parker, you know we have a few days to work on your tree fort, so how about you take it easy when we get you back to your grandparents?"

"Mr. Lloyd, maybe I will. I think I need to take a little nap when we get home. Will you wait for me until I wake up? Then we can unload the truck."

As Lloyd headed onto the road, he watched Parker take his new hammer from the seat and placed it on his lap, holding it with both hands. Gently patting the top of Parker's head, Lloyd said in reassuring tones, "Hey there big boy, you bet I will wait for you! You and I are a team!"

His young partner then closed his eyes and rested his body against Lloyd. By the time they arrived at Klem and Jane's, little Parker was so sound asleep that Lloyd decided to carry him into their house. He carefully parked his truck as smoothly as possible and placed the shifter into "park." Before he was able to quietly open his driver's side door, Abby came out to greet them. As she caught Lloyd's eye, her heart quickened, and she felt her breathing increasing. It seemed to happen whenever she was close to him again, and occasionally, even when she just thought about Lloyd.

With a smile, Lloyd rolled down his driver's window, which Abby understood as an invitation to give him a kiss through the opening. The light perfume from her recently applied lipstick and the touch of her delicate lips delivered a sensual shiver down Lloyd's back. Hungry for another blissful kiss, he gently touched the side of her tan, freckled face and received another.

"So, my carpenter man-friend, you plumb wore out my son. Did you?"

She paused for a few seconds and said with a cute, playful smile, "You could have done at least *some* of the work yourself instead of making poor Parker do it all by himself!"

With that, she gave Lloyd an approving and understanding wink, then walked to the passenger side to scoop Parker into her arms.

"Lloyd, are you going to the monthly community meeting tonight? If you are planning to go, I will allow you to escort me there and back. In fact, if you play your cards right, I will let you sit next to me. Well...do you fancy that invitation? Be careful how you answer, Mr. Gazebo Builder, this is a limited time offer!"

"Abby dear, if you are going, I am fully in. I will present myself at this very porch tonight at 6:30 sharp."

"You better be here. I will be wearing my blue L.L.Bean hat so you can find me easier. See you then!"

Still holding Parker in her arms, she gave her wink and an air kiss, then turned to the screen door while humming softly.

Parker opened his sleepy eyes when Abby took him upstairs and into his bed. She softly kissed his cheek and spoke to him with a gentle whisper, "Tonight, during the community meeting, our neighbor Silvia will come over to our home to be with you."

Parker made an approving murmur and rolled over onto his side. Within a half a minute, he was asleep.

CHAPTER
4

A Community Meeting

True to his word, Lloyd stepped onto her porch exactly at the appointed time. Even before knocking, Abby came out with Klem and Jane accompanying her. Klem greeted Lloyd with a hardy handshake and then said, "Don't worry about us. You can walk with Abby…Jane and I will be just behind a few paces. That way, I might steal a kiss from my favorite Port James squeeze."

"Now, Klem my magnificent husband of forty-nine years, I better be your *only* Port James squeeze!"

With that exchange, the foursome turned to the Victorian gaslit sidewalk and walked the four blocks to the village hall meeting room. Without Abby and Lloyd knowing, when strolling past each streetlight, Klem gave Jane a kiss. Each time Klem got his kiss from Jane, he placed a quarter in her hand.

The village hall sported a modified Greek facade having three wide granite steps that lead to the entrance. Above the doors were the words carved in stone "Port James" and underneath this "Maine's Seaside Village." Inside was a grouping of seventy wooden chairs having an arrangement of seven rows with ten chairs in each row. Klem, Jane, Abby, and Lloyd found four empty chairs together and sat down. As they settled in, those already in attendance turned around in their seats and acknowledged them with either a smile or a head nod. Out of tradition and respect, the men took off their hats and placed them either on their laps or hung them on the backs of their chairs.

After a few more minutes, Sarah, the meeting coordinator, stepped up to the raised stage. While standing at the podium, she organized her papers. Promptly at seven o'clock, she tapped the microphone with her finger. Satisfied that it was working, she said, "Welcome, everyone, to this month's Port James community meeting. We should be done with our business portion fairly soon as long as no one has anything more they need to bring up tonight. If you are able, please let us all stand for the *Pledge of Allegiance.*"

After everyone sat back down and adjusted their chairs, Sarah placed her bifocals on the bridge of her nose. Tilting her paper a little to see it better, she addressed the first item of business.

"Again, welcome and thank you all for coming. First of all, has anyone seen the finished gazebo at our village park on First Avenue and Maple? My walk always takes me through the park, and I almost had a tear in my eye. It is simply beautiful as well as stately. As you all know, our local woodworker, Lloyd, built the entire structure from the bottom up, so to speak. In fact, I know he also designed it and presented his plans to the board for approval just two months ago…I think it was April 2, and now it is all done! How nice is that? Lloyd, could you please stand?"

Lloyd looked a little surprised, then released his hand from Abby's and stood up.

"I just wanted everyone to give Lloyd an applause, but first, I wish to say that he did such a great job, no, I *mean a great job!* Lloyd, during my walks, I saw that you started even when there was quite a bit of snow on the ground. I wondered if you could even feel your fingertips. So let's all give Lloyd an applause."

As Lloyd stood there a little sheepishly, the attendees in the whole room all stood up and, with wild enthusiasm, gave him a standing ovation. This never happened to him before. In fact, the reward he received was doing his best with his gazebo building. After what felt like five minutes, even though it was only a half a minute, he sat back down to see Abby looking so proud of him. She was glowing all over with admiration.

The attendees saw Sarah readjust her eye glasses, then flip to her next page. Continuing on, she then said, "Okay, now on to our scheduled agenda. This next one is a request from one of our elderly gentlemen residents. He is not here today, so I agreed to speak for him. Mr. Grumy, as some of you might know, lives on Fourth Street and Maple Avenue. It is that large white corner home with a matching white picket fence all around his property. Well, some neighborhood boys who travel by foot to and from school have taken to finding a stick to rub along the pickets while they walk. I am told that it makes such a pleasant noise. Well, a pleasant noise for young boys. All this is to say that each time they do this, they kind of make scratch marks on Mr. Grumy's white fence.

"On one day when the boys were doing this, it happens to be when Mr. Grumy was having breakfast. He came out with porridge on his face. Or was it gruel on his face? Anyway, he came storming out of his house to yell at the boys. Well, my friends, it was reported that he terrified the boys somewhat silly. They dropped their sticks and ran all the way home. So after that, they made sure to never miss the opportunity repeat this activity every time.

"I believe they thought it was even more fun after Mr. Grumy chased them. So I guess I am asking if you happen to see this going on, please kindly ask the boys to refrain from this habit. Is everyone comfortable with that?"

Sarah looked around the room and did not see anyone objecting. She placed both outstretched arms on her podium and then took in a large breath. Exhaling slowly, she continued, "All right... now for the third announcement for consideration. This involves our unleashed dogs around town. Please, please, please honor and follow our leash laws, that is, for our dogs, not little boys. Ha! Ha!"

Sarah was not one to make humorous or witty comments, so being proud of herself, she waited for chuckles then continued on, "This one is about one of our cherished businesses in town. There were a few unfortunate instances that happened at Beth's Bakery. Now we all know that Beth loves puppies. Right, Beth?"

Beth was sitting in the front row and gave a little nod in agreement. Sarah waited a few seconds and continued along, "In fact, I know that every morning, Beth always sets out a bowl of fresh water on the sidewalk for these little creatures. The issue is that a few times, several dogs have ventured inside her bakery. As quick as a mermaid's wink, they jump up on the bread cooling rack when Beth is working in the back. They managed to steal a whole loaf of warm French bread. Maybe it is Italian, but whatever bread it was, out the door the dogs went, as fast as their legs could go.

"Some of the dock workers at the wharf have seen these dogs tearing into the freshly baked bread with seagulls scooping up the larger crumbs. Of course, we all know that those darn seagulls leave their droppings everywhere, creating quite a mess. It makes it very unpleasant for those walking along the docks. Their white poop is probably unsanitary as well. Oh, I am on a tangent. Now, where was I? Oh yes, the bread-stealing dogs. So can we all make sure our little four-legged friends stay on leashes? Enough said? Great, now proceeding on.

"I guess tonight's meeting is somewhat heavy with dog topics. So here it goes…agenda item number four. Next month, on June 20, is the *Annual Balancing Stone Competition*. Some of us call this the *Stacking Stone Competition*, but you all know what I mean. We all love this festival since five years ago, George and Carmen who own *Tinker's Country Kitchen* restaurant have supplied the food. They always steam plenty of one-and-a-quarter-pound lobsters, salt potatoes, and buttered corn for such a reasonable price. Personally, I don't know how they make any money, but they look forward to doing it.

"Now back to the rocks. Some of those balancing works of art…well…all of them in fact were perfectly unbelievable. I believe a few of them were all of ten feet high.

"However, friends. Unknown to most during this festival last year, a few of our local dogs decided these artworks would be a perfect place to lift their legs. To use a phrase that we all know, it put a damper on the whole festival. It wouldn't have been so bad except the photo coverage on the first page of the newspaper unintentionally caught the canine relieving himself on one of tallest balancing rocks.

That particular balancing rock piece was sponsored by the Senior Citizen's Center. So once again if you bring your dogs, could we make sure they are on a restraining leash? Good people, thank you very much."

Klem looked at Jane, then Jane started to laugh. It was a little giggle at first; then, she just couldn't stifle it. Her whole body was shaking as she pinched her nose with her fingers, which of course led Klem to start laughing. He tried to look away to help, but it wasn't to be. Instead, he blurted out what was supposed to be only a whisper but, because of his laughing, came out like a megaphone.

"I think it was most fortunate that the dog didn't knock the whole darn thing on top of one of the senior citizens."

Sarah pretended that she did not hear Klem's comment but decided to enjoy it as well. She then promptly closed the meeting for the evening. Most of the older men who were present thought this was the best community meeting that they had ever attended.

On the walk home, Jane tried to scold her hubby but decided to let it go. After walking a few blocks, Lloyd bent over toward Abby and whispered, "I had no idea that your dad had that funny side. I truly think that is pretty cool."

CHAPTER 5

A Life-Changing Letter

It was one of those regular, normal days that anyone would have thought was uneventful, but those things cannot always be planned in one's life. It started out with Lloyd and Parker placing some more wood pieces on the tree fort. While Abby sat in the backyard, she had a ringside seat of the construction process. At the same time, a short distance away, she could enjoy a beautiful view of Port James lighthouse.

That lighthouse was her dad's pride and joy. Over the years, Klem had walked the footpath from his house at least twenty thousand times to tend Port James lighthouse. The lawn needed mowing once a week, and the flowers asked for their catering to as well. From time to time, the white stucco exterior needed patching and painting, but the most important duty was keeping the lifesaving light beam operational.

In years past, the wick inside the fourth order lens was fueled with kerosene that had to be replenished daily. It also had to be wound every twenty hours. In 1999, the Fresnel lens was replaced with an electrical light and motor. Even with that improvement, the lamp house windows at the top of the railing and deck still needed cleaning because of the salt air and the seagulls.

Sipping her coffee, then looking up, it warmed Abby's heart as she listened to Lloyd's gentle voice giving Parker helpful directions.

"See, Parker, try not to swing your hammer by moving your wrist. Use your whole arm instead. You will last a lot longer without getting so tired. See? Try it on this next nail...that's it, partner...you got it!"

With every day that passed, Parker was growing closer and closer to his friend. Not that he would ever forget his dad, but he really needed a male figure in his little life. Lately, Parker could not keep up with the energy of his neighborhood friends who were his own age. It wasn't their fault, but they would usually leave him behind while continuing whatever activity they were doing. Parker longed to bike or run with them on the beaches to chase seagulls.

So on this day, out on the front sidewalk, Ben, the mailman, was walking his normal route. Pausing at their mailbox, he reached into his leather pouch and placed a letter inside along with an assortment of fliers. That particular letter had a postmark stamped from New York City. The letter was addressed to Abby. Ben closed the mailbox door and continued on to their neighbors.

At the same time, Abby took a look at her watch. She got up from her chaise lounge and walked over to the construction site.

"Hey, boys. Do either of you want something to drink? I am going to check on the mail."

Parker yelled down from the tree and said they still have some unopened bottled water, so they were okay.

"Well, my hardworking guys, in about an hour, I think Parker will probably want to take a nap. Is that right, Parker?"

Lloyd answered for him by saying that they will probably stop before that time. Abby stood there and asked a few more questions about the tree fort before walking around the house to get the mail.

When Abby got to the mailbox, she opened its door and reached in to retrieve the contents. Closing the door, she started to flip through the various letters. There were advertising fliers, an electric bill, and lastly, the letter addressed to her. Separating her own letter, she took the rest of the mail bundle to the front porch. Arriving on the entryway, she placed all the mail in a pile on top of the white wicker end table. Still standing, she opened her letter and started to read. After the first sentence, she took three steps to the Adirondack chair and sat down.

> *Dear Abby,*
> *Can you believe it has been four years since...*

Abby finished the letter and looked up at the seagulls soaring through the clouds. Here in her hand was a message that made her mind whirl. For so many reasons, she was not ready for its message. She thought, *How could one piece of paper in a nondescript envelope change my life so dramatically?* With shaking hands, she folded the letter in thirds and placed it into her pants pocket.

Not now, but sometime later, she would have to deal with it.

When she turned around, she saw Lloyd walking toward her while using his hands to bang sawdust from his pants.

"Hey, beautiful! I think Parker is ready for a nap. I took him inside through the back door where his grandmother received him. I think she took him upstairs for his rest. You know, I don't have to tell you this, but I just have to say that he is one terrific lad. I really love being with him. Parker is so eager to practically learn everything. You should be proud of him. He has pretty good control over his new hammer. Parker must have pounded thirty or more nails today."

Lloyd looked a little pensive, then reached for Abby's hand.

"Say, I wanted to ask you a question...I was hoping for a *yes* from you, but either way, I understand. I have at least one whole week before my next project, which is an attached gazebo for Brent and Christine Thompson's home. So I am kind of free for the next few days."

For at least the time being, the impact of this morning's letter took second place to Lloyd's attempt to ask her something. It seemed that Lloyd had a little trouble fishing for his words. A few times, he started his question to Abby, then stopped and then started again.

"Lloyd! For crying out in the great blue ocean surf! I am so very glad that you enjoy Parker's company. It means more than you know. But can you please get to your request for me?"

"Oh yes, as I was saying, would you like to share a day in Portland tomorrow or this Wednesday? We could spend several hours and return the same day since it is only an hour's drive. What do you think, honey?"

To Lloyd's surprise, Abby launched off the two porch steps and flew into his arms, with her legs wrapped tightly around his waist. Lloyd felt his heartbeat pound with the same excited rhythm of Abby's. Still coupled together, they twirled around three times in the front yard; then, they both fell together onto the soft grass. Their lips touched each other's; then, they kissed passionately. Lloyd looked into Abby's ocean blue sparkling eyes and said, "I will take that to mean you are free to go! Right?"

Abby giggled a few times as they both untwined their bodies and carefully got back onto their feet. She adjusted her hair behind her ears and smoothed out her blouse with her hands.

"Well, my handsome man-friend, what time tomorrow do you want me to be ready?"

Unknown to Abby and Lloyd, Klem and Jane were viewing the entire outside acrobatics. As they watched from the front room, Jane was standing with her half-filled teacup in her hand. Klem, who was sitting, had placed his book down just in time. Jane set her cup on the end table next to her husband's book and said, "Klem, does that bring back any memories about when we were quite a little bit younger? You were always wanting to grab me and give me a hug."

Klem slowly eased up from his leather reclining chair and touched his woman's shoulders. He enjoyed looking at her soft complexion, her expressive eyes, and her beautiful silver white hair. With gentleness mixed with fun, he said, "Well, my little mermaid, that hasn't changed a bit. I am certainly ready for my morning hug!"

CHAPTER 6

A Trip to Portland

Singing a little tune, Lloyd got into his truck and drove toward Abby's home. Viewing the blue sky through his windshield, he was pleased that it looked like a perfect day to tour a city. From time to time, he glanced at his dancing dashboard hula girl. She seemed to be smiling back at him. Since no one else was in his truck, Lloyd felt he could "talk" with the little painted plastic figure.

"Hey, little hula girl, you and I have been through a lot together. Right now, I can hardly believe that Abby and I are an item. I love to be with her, and she seems to love me too! All my life I have devoted so much time to building gazebos and other wood structures that I have not thought about dating. Well, that's not entirely true. I think about it a lot, but I always have a customer on my list that wants something else built."

Lloyd slowed his truck down to a stop to wait for a red traffic light to change. As little Hula momentarily stopped dancing, she seemed to be thinking about his words.

"Yes, Hula, I know it is all my fault. I work too hard to find time to date. As you know, I love woodworking. But now, God seemed to have blessed me a hundredfold with Abby's precious friendship. Little Hula, don't be jealous. You will always have a special place in my heart. As far as Abby, I love her looks, her jet-black hair, and ocean blue eyes and soft freckled sun-kissed skin. She also has an innocence about her, I guess like I probably have. All I know is that it seemed that God has made my gazebo-building muscles shaped perfectly to hold her in my arms just right. Ha! I knew my hard-working bicep muscles of mine would come in handy for more than pounding nails."

By this time, the traffic light changed to green, and little Hula started dancing again, which Lloyd interpreted as her accepting Abby. Within a few short minutes, Lloyd was pulling into the Watercrest's driveway. His heart started racing when he saw Abby coming down the front porch steps to greet him.

"Hi there, Mr. Gazebo Builder, who has finally and graciously scheduled some getaway time for us!"

Abby opened the truck passenger door and slid over to feel Lloyd's lips once again on hers.

"My oh my! You big hunk! You look good and smell great in your tight jeans and muscle shirt!"

Lloyd was flashing his generous smile from ear to ear. He then decided to add some humor.

"Did you say that I look good, but *I smell great?* Don't I *look great* too?"

"Well, my macho carpenter, yes, you do look great. Now how about me? What do you think?"

Lloyd looked at her pretty face smiling at him and said, "I was just going to say that you look as cute as my little dancing hula girl."

* * * * *

Lloyd found that Portland had a three-story parking garage a few blocks from the waterfront. However, as luck would have it, he located a parking spot with a meter on the street, which was right by the water. Lloyd had been to Portland a few times to replace some of the wood planks on their boardwalk, but it was the first time for Abby. After checking her lipstick in the visor mirror, she pushed it back up and said, "Wow! What a great spot you found to park! I will let you take full advantage of your parking talent by allowing you to escort me along the water!"

Abby got out of the truck and looked at the harbor while Lloyd fed the parking meter with some coins. The weather was perfect, boasting an ocean breeze, blue sky, and just right for wearing a light jacket. On one side of them were commercial boats of different dimensions, and across the street, all sorts of fun shops to visit. After walking hand in hand while taking in the ocean air, Abby said, "Thanks for wanting to spend time with me, my man-friend. This is already so much fun. While we were walking, I was just wondering, did you bring any money? If so, let's go across the street and check out some shops! You just might want to buy me something!"

The two friends visited shops of every kind. One shop had every kind of kitchen cooking utensils imaginable. Down a ways was a fun store for both youngsters and adults alike. The only items that were sold were beautiful kites of all sizes. A good number of the kites were hanging from the ceiling, which made them appear like they were flying. Lloyd couldn't fathom how some of the more unusual-shaped kites could ever stay in the air. Abby was mesmerized at the bright colors and patterns that each one had. It seemed to her that every kite was trying to outdo each other.

Another little shop sold only beer, wine, and a variety of cheese and crackers. Upon entering, Lloyd could not help himself from looking upwards at the huge natural wood beams that held up the tongue and groove plank ceiling. He estimated the ceiling height to be twenty or more feet. Strolling around some more, Lloyd noticed the store's wide windowsills. The nearest one to him was occupied by a kitty. The tiger cat was catching some warm sunshine that was streaming through the window. Lloyd looked around and saw what he believed to be the store proprietor. The gentleman wore a brown-bibbed work-apron and sported a well-trimmed pure white beard. He displayed an approving smile while walking toward Lloyd.

"Hi there, my friend. My name is Vern, and this is my shop. However, my kitty…his name is Captain, thinks he is the real owner. If you wish, Captain will be happy to receive a little massage from you."

Without hesitation, Lloyd went over to the window and the captain. He rubbed its back several times then the top of his head. Captain seemed to enjoy the attention and reacted with a singing purr. After a minute, Vern said, "I notice that you were analyzing my ceiling. Fifteen years ago, when I was searching to buy a business here in Portland, I looked very closely at eight properties that were listed for sale. To tell you the truth, the ceiling in this one sold me."

Lloyd said, "Yes, the natural wood with oak beams are truly magnificent. You made the right choice including this kitty of yours."

"I see you also know your wood, my friend. Hey! Are you from out of town and visiting our fine city of Portland?"

By this time, Abby joined the two men, sliding her hand in Lloyd's. Lloyd said, "By the way, my name is Lloyd, and this is Abby."

He extended his arm for a handshake and gave a smile.

"Why, yes, my woman-friend and I are just visiting for the day. Why do you ask?"

"There is something that I think you would be quite interested in visiting. It is a little ways away from where most vacationers tour. It is called the *Portland Observatory*. I could tell you more, but if you go, I will let the tour guide tell you. It is located on Munjoy Hill. Since it is a little ways away, you should take your car. Hey, nice meeting you both, and I hope you enjoy Portland."

Even though they visited quite a few shops along the harbor, there was one particular store that Abby loved. To Lloyd's surprise, it was an old-fashioned hardware store. This was also Lloyd's favorite, but he could not believe that Abby thoroughly enjoyed exploring every aisle of the store. Skipping ahead, Abby turned around and excitingly announced, "Look here, Lloyd! Look at this display! There must be fifty or sixty kinds of different drawer knobs!"

Lloyd stepped away from where he was examining new leather utility belts. He could see that she was excited about rows and rows of display bins. Standing in front of the bins, Abby was in awe with both the variety and quality of hardware knobs. One after another, she took them in her hand and held each one up to the ceiling lights. Some knobs were made of cut glass and others were painted ceramic. The glass ones caught the ceiling light and made beautiful spectrums of colorful patterns. Some of the ceramic knobs were the shapes of sailboats, ship wheels, lobsters, and whales. One looked like a compass with north, south, east, and west printed on it. What really caught Abby's eye were lighthouse knobs. The set included drawer pulls that were in the shape of long ocean waves.

"Lloyd, just look at all of these knobs and drawer pulls! I can't believe it! I have been looking for something that Parker would like in his bedroom. His dresser is functional but kind of boring. He would just love these."

She found a table where she placed the lighthouse knobs in five rows of two each along with corresponding drawer pulls. She tucked her black hair behind her ears with her fingers, then looked a little more at her arrangement. After some more contemplation, she turned to Lloyd and asked, "My manly date, do you know how you could impress this little lady of yours?"

"I thought you would never ask."

"I would love you to the ends of the ocean if you bought these for Parker. What do you think? I believe it is a great deal for you!"

Lloyd touched her cheek and asked, "To the ends of the ocean? How could I refuse that offer?"

CHAPTER 7

The Portland Observatory

Both Abby and Lloyd could hardly believe that they had already been touring Portland for five hours. Each had packages of new treasures in their hands. The one brown bag Lloyd carried had the utility belt he purchased from the hardware store. In Abby's arms was a box that had the set of nautical dresser drawer pulls and knobs for Parker's bedroom. Abby was beaming knowing that her son will get a nice gift and her man had a new belt to replace his old one.

By this time, both friends were more than just a little hungry. They walked a little more slowly every time they passed a restaurant. Lloyd was the first one to talk about where they should go for lunch.

"My little getaway friend, what kind of food do you fancy for today?"

"Did you call me a getaway friend? Well, I will take that as a compliment. You know, I think we should have seafood. However, just as importantly, I would also love to eat near one of those piers so we can watch the water activity while we eat."

They walked a little longer, then strolled out to a pier that looked like there were several nautical restaurants to choose from. They found one overlooking the water called Captain Moody's. Lloyd opened the door for his lady, and once inside, they noticed that the restaurant boasted of a pirate's décor. Most tables and booths were full of patrons eating their lunch or having a mixed drink. As if standing with them to wait for a table was a full-sized female pirate with a low-cut cream-colored ruffled blouse. It was perfectly carved out of wood and painted authentically including the parrot bird on her left shoulder. The ceiling had fishnets hanging from the beams, which were artistically filled with multicolored floating glass balls. The side walls were made of dark wood clapboard and had several brass portholes. The far end of the restaurant was a series of generous windows that overlooked boats cruising past in both directions.

Just as their eyes were getting used to the darker light, the hostess welcomed them and asked if they wished to be near the windows. She invited them to follow her to a table that had a nice view of the water. When seated, Wendy, the waitress, offered them the menu and asked if they wanted anything to drink. Responding to Abby and Lloyd that water would be fine, she said, "Coming right up, skipper and first mate! I'll be right back to take your order."

Both of them chuckled a little because of the names she called them; then, they lightly disagreed as to who was the skipper and who was the first mate. After a few minutes, Wendy delivered their ice water in thick glass beer mugs and took their meal orders. After ordering, but before letting her go, Abby asked Wendy if she knew why the restaurant was named Captain Moody.

"Oh yes! Captain Moody was the gentleman that organized the construction of an observatory tower, right here in Portland. If you have the time, I would recommend going to it."

At the same moment, Lloyd and Abby both said that it certainly was their afternoon plan. Within a short time, Wendy came loaded down with two steaming deep-dish plates. When she placed both in front of them, she offered, "Eat hearty, mates, and enjoy! Just yell out to me if you need anything."

The lunch made both of them roll their eyes with delight. It was a light clear sautéed seafood melody of scallops, clams, shrimp, and lobster placed on a bed of hardy mashed potatoes. The two of them enjoyed the scrumptious food, wonderful view, and their closeness that happens when two lovers care so much for each other.

Wendy came back and asked if they wanted dessert.

"We have a mermaid's laugh, which is a seven-layer white cake with vanilla ice cream; high tide, which is apple pie; and whale's tail, a blue-colored sherbet."

Both of them declined because they were so full; then, Wendy said she expected that would be true. Very few of her customers needed anything more after eating the seafood melody. When paying the cashier, Wendy gave a big wave and a captain's salute, telling them to come back soon.

* * * * *

It was just a short drive up to Munjoy Hill, the location of the Portland Observatory Tower. When Lloyd parked and opened Abby's door for her, he looked up and almost tripped over his feet. The structure was both stately and more immense than he could have imagined. Abby took his hand and slid from her seat.

"Goodness, Lloyd, I thought that I was the only thing that swept you off your feet, but I have to admit, this is pretty impressive. Hopefully, it is still open so we can go to the top. Let's go over there and see!"

As the two hurried to the little ticket booth, Scott, the observatory's tour guide, waved to them to come up to where he was standing.

"Hi, folks, you are just in time to get into my last tour. In fact, you two lucky people will be the only ones this time. So greetings, and welcome to Portland's Observatory Tower. Since you are over twelve but a long ways from sixty-five years old, that will be five dollars each."

Lloyd gave him a ten spot, and Scott handed him two souvenir admission tickets.

"Okay, thank you very much, folks. I am happy to see that you both have reasonable shoes to climb up to the top. Some lady tourists come here in spiked high heels. Can you imagine that, spiked heels, really? Now before we start up to the top, let me tell you some interesting facts about this majestic lady."

35

The three of them were standing by the entrance while Scott started his memorized informational talk. Lloyd couldn't help himself from repeatedly looking upward to the top of the structure with total amazement. Scott noticed Lloyd's admiration for the skill that was required to construct this structure and said, "Son, by the look in your eyes, I wonder if you work in wood for a living. Well, let me tell you about its history. A man named Captain Lemuel Moody organized to have this observatory tower constructed in 1807.

"See, Portland's harbor is sheltered by several islands. Even now, any boat, ship, or vessel coming into port are not visible from the wharfs. So back then, if you were a merchant, you had a very short time to prepare for the arrival of your cargo when the vessel carrying your cargo finally appeared. Of course, back then, they did not have any radio communications.

"Because of Captain Moody's efforts, this observatory was built. With the use of a telescope at the top, ships could be sighted and identified up to thirty miles at sea. This gave a 'heads-up' to the merchants several hours before the ship reached the docks. They used signal flags that they hoisted from the top. It was a fairly efficient two-way communication between the ship, the shore hands, and the merchants.

"Now let me tell you about some construction details of this lovely lady. She is eighty-six feet tall, which is as tall as a seven-story building of today. It is octagonal, which means it is eight-sided and has a fieldstone base of heavy loose rocks. The top is two hundred and twenty-two feet above sea level. As you climb it, you will notice the eight massive beams. Each beam starts way down among the loose rocks below the ground and stretch skyward all the way to the top. Each of these supporting beams are made of one single piece of wood. The staircase that you will climb is attached to the inside wall. Typical spiral staircases found in lighthouses are located in the middle and are attached and supported by a metal pole. So now, let me open the door, and you can start your ascent to the observation deck."

Lloyd wondered if Abby was a little nervous to climb the staircase, but she took his hand and excitedly started with him by her side. As they went along, Scott gave a few more details.

"During the War of 1812, this observatory tower actually served as a lookout for invading British warships. In 1972, it was placed on the *National Register of Historic Places*, and in 2006, it was designated a *national historical landmark.*"

Scott stopped halfway up to catch his breath and turned around to make sure his audience was keeping up.

"I might not have mentioned that fees were collected from shipping merchants who purchased flags for the tower's use. These flags were stored in the building and hoisted up at the observation deck from poles when their ships were sighted. Okay, we are almost there. When we arrive at the top and if you venture outside, please hold onto the outside railing at all times. I haven't yet had anyone flip over it and free fall to the ground, and I don't want it to ever happen… especially to such a fine couple as you two."

Lloyd and Abby took a moment to catch their breath, then entered the round observation room. Taking each other's hands, they excitingly went through the small door to the outside railing. Holding the black iron railing in her left hand and her other hand tightly holding Lloyd's, the two stood in complete silence. Just below them was the magnificent city of Portland. They had a bird's-eye view of the same streets they walked along and some of the shops they visited. Most of the buildings were totally made of red brick giving a pleasing monochromatic appearance.

Further out and past the buildings, they both saw and felt a small wisp of fog slowly coming toward the shore. The tide was coming in, as if to announce the start of evening. For one last trip of the day, seagulls were catching wind currents, turning their heads from left to right in search of a dinner. A few gulls were still following a boat or two as they cut their motors to slow their speed toward the night docks.

Lloyd and Abby allowed the silence to speak for them for a while, extending this beautiful tranquility. Time melted away, and they were treated to the very beginning of God's awesome sunset.

Trying not to disturb them, Scott opened the door from inside just a few inches. Peeking through the open-door crack, he whispered to them with an understanding tone in his voice, "I see that you enjoy this view as much as I have over the years. Plus, I think you are a special couple that need this time together. Since you two are the only ones here, I can let you remain up here for a while. I will be going back down because there are a few more things that need attending in the ticket booth. So take your time, and I will meet you outside at the base."

Abby thanked him for his perceptiveness and assured him that they would be descending the staircase within a short period of time. Scott nodded and reclosed the door. As the colors in the sky silently started to glow around them, Abby took her hand off the railing and held her man in both of his. Ever so quietly, and sincerely, she whispered, "Lloyd, thank you for today, and thank you for being you."

CHAPTER
8

Parker, Lloyd, and Abby

Jane and Abby were once again gathered around the breakfast table. This time, however, Klem decided to make his famous egg omelet for his family. First of all, he found his wife's black-and-white checkered apron on her wooden hook and put it on. Jane saw he was having trouble tying the apron strings on his backside. So after a few minutes, she got up and tied it for him.

"Thank you, my good lady. I truly do not know how you womenfolk tie things behind your backs all by yourselves. Besides, when I watch you tie it, you make it look so easy. But now, scoot! This morning, I am the master chef in our kitchen."

Klem retrieved eight eggs from the refrigerator, and with a technique that he saw on the food channel, he broke them on the side of a deep glass mixing bowl. He then added some fresh cream, a pinch of salt, onion powder, and garlic powder. Next, he introduced a full cup of grilled bacon bits that he had prepared the night before. Finishing the ingredients was some chopped sweet red and green peppers.

With a metal wire whisk, he mixed it until fluffy. Singing the church hymn "When the Saints Come Marching In," he poured his creation into a deep-frying pan that had been glazed with melted butter. At the right time, he folded it over and sectioned them on prewarmed breakfast plates.

By this time, the breakfast aroma had awakened Parker who came down the stairs and into the kitchen. Rubbing his eyes after a large yawn, Parker found his chair and sat down. Looking at everyone's omelets, he said, "We should thank God for making eggs, and I also want to thank you, Grandpa, for making this breakfast! I need to have a hearty meal like this one today because Lloyd and I are going to the Port James Marine Museum that just opened down at the wharf. We could easily walk there, but Lloyd said that we will take his truck."

In a few minutes, Parker was done eating. He then took his plate and silverware into the kitchen to put on the counter next to the sink.

"Mom, after I brush my teeth, if it is all right with you, can I wait for Lloyd on the front porch?"

Abby collected the remaining place settings and said it would be fine as long as he also combed his hair while he was in the bathroom. A short time later, Lloyd's truck was heard through the screen door. Abby couldn't wait for him to come inside, so she hurried outside to greet him. She met him on the front porch and delivered a nice morning kiss on his lips.

"Hi there, man of my dreams! Goodness, gracious me! Parker is so excited that you are taking him to the new marine museum. Thank you for being so kind to him, he really admires you."

"Well, you should know by now that I really love that little guy. I will have him back home in a few hours, unless he gets tired sooner."

By that time, Parker came bouncing out of the house with a little leftover toothpaste still on his lips. The two guys got into the truck and headed down the hill to the docks. Within six minutes, they were inside the museum, looking at what it had to offer.

* * * * *

It had been only two hours when the men came back to the house. Parker excitingly ran inside, holding a colorful brochure with pictures of some of the displays. Jane and Abby were sitting on the front room couch together, looking through an L.L.Bean summer catalog. Parker jumped on the sofa between them. Pointing to the pictures, he said, "Look, Mom, look, Grandma, it was so much fun! They had a shallow tank where I could actually pick up a live starfish and pet a real sea skate! Oh, there was also a leatherback turtle. It feeds on migratory jellyfish when it comes up here from North Carolina. There was a real schooner ship that I could go on with Lloyd. It was inside the museum, and even though it didn't move, it was real cool. I went up to the captain's bridge and actually tooted the horn!

"The best part was a barrel of seawater. Lloyd picked me up so I could see what was inside. Do you know what it was? I couldn't believe my eyes! There were hundreds of baby lobsters, newly hatched...Lloyd told me. The amazing thing...are you ready for this? They were so very tiny, about as small as...hmm...well smaller than a dime, and they looked just like a large lobster only smaller! Oh, another thing about those baby lobsters, you could see right through them!"

Abby looked at her child's happy demure with such appreciation.

"It sure sounds like you two travelers had a great time. Thanks again, Lloyd, for taking him. Maybe someday, you will take me. How about it?"

Lloyd smiled, then excused himself so that he could meet a potential customer about building a small storage shed in his backyard. Abby then said that Parker should have some lunch followed by taking his nap.

For this morning, all is good with the world.

CHAPTER 9

Abby's Birthday Present

It was early in the morning, and Lloyd was very aware that he was too excited to lay in bed any longer. Since the early edition had arrived at his home at 4:00 a.m., he decided to get up, start the Keurig coffee maker, then retrieve the newspaper from the front yard.

Briefly scanning the headlines as he went back into his house, Lloyd was greeted with the nice aroma of his hot flavored coffee. The coffee maker had automatically filled his cup, so with his cup in hand and paper under his arm, he walked over to his table and sat down. He placed the paper aside and looked at the plans he had started the night before. It was the shed for the Jackson's. Constructing simple sheds made him money, and he built them very well, but they were kind of boring. With this project, for some reason, they wanted the shed to look like a train depot. This delighted Lloyd since it would be quite involved, and he liked the challenge.

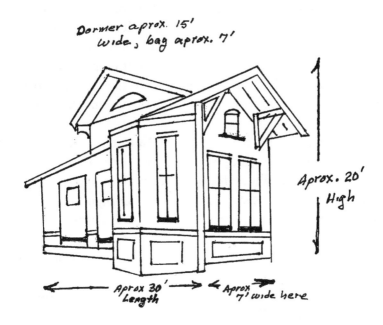

Dormer aprox. 15'
wide, bag aprox. 7'

Aprox. 20'
High

Aprox 30'
Length

Aprox 7' wide here

He set the plans aside and took a sweet roll from a bakery box next to him. He remembered another reason to be excited. For the last few weeks, Abby had hinted that today would be her birthday. Since she gave him ample time to think about a present, he thought of a superb one to give her.

A few days ago, while working on a gracious and cascading outside staircase, he took the time to call Port James Sailing Rentals. After talking a little, the lady on the phone wanted to make sure that before renting, the customer had ample experience in the sport. Lloyd assured her, and so she reserved a Sunfish for three hours on the day he asked for.

In this early morning, Lloyd allowed his mind to retrace the enjoyment he had while listening to Abby. She always had an enthusiastic voice whenever she was telling him about sailing during her college years. He learned from her that a friend named Terri shared the same love of this sport. Since they were roommates at college, when not studying, they were planning their next sailing outing.

He seemed to remember that Abby referred to them as *single-handed*, meaning that she was solely responsible for managing all the wind and wave forces. Both she and Terri loved that idea and enjoyed the learning process to master the sailing skills.

It took them several sailing outings, but eventually, they knew how to tackle, just like an experienced pro. Lloyd took another sip of java and continued to recall more conversations they had about sailing.

"Tackling," Abby had explained, "means mastering the sail directions to use the wind to move forward and steer. Using a zigzag pattern, you can actually go forward even with the wind against you. I think that is incredible. Of course, when changing the sail direction, you just better duck or get hit on the head. During my first few attempts, I got pushed completely into the water by the boom."

On many occasions, when Abby and Lloyd went out together, they would find a place to sit on the rocks near the ocean. Most of the time, it was at the Port James lighthouse. Looking at the playful waves, Abby would talk in between each crash, happy to be near the ocean that seemed to be laughing with them.

Remembering some more of Abby's sailing experiences from college, he also recalled her saying, "I prefer the Sunfish brand, but Terri grew to like the Aero sailboats. She liked having a clear plastic section on her sails so she could look through it. I don't know. I never cared about that."

Lloyd took another sip of his coffee and then allowed himself to remember additional conversations when he and Abby sat at the ocean's edge.

"Now, I would not go into ocean water like where we are now, but I liked it when the wind would get strong enough in the inlets to make it a challenge. Oh, am I boring you, my love?"

"Absolutely not, I could listen to you for hours. You have such sparkle in your eyes when you talk about sailing. Could you tell me about the various parts of a one-person sailboat?"

Lloyd was asking to learn something but more to totally enjoy her expressions.

"Well, honey, there is the rudder that steers the boat. See, that is attached to the tiller, which is a stick so to speak, that you hold onto. The tiller is used to go left and right, just like the steering wheel of a car. Then there is the boom, which is the pole on the bottom of the sail, and of course, the mast. Oh! I could go on forever, but I don't want to bore you, my man."

Still sitting at his kitchen table, Lloyd blinked his eyes a few times and finished his daydreaming. Enjoying the taste of his sweet roll, he decided that he was completely pleased with his birthday present for Abby. He looked at the time on his cellphone and noticed that he had better take his shower and get dressed to get to her house on time.

CHAPTER
10

Sail Away

Lloyd hardly had time to stop his truck in the Watercrest's driveway before both Parker and Abby came running up to him.

He managed to open his driver's door just in time to get hugs from each of them. Parker was jumping up and down, saying, "Today is my mom's birthday, her birthday, her birthday! We will be having cake and ice cream for dessert after dinner tonight!"

After this greeting, Parker danced off, and back into the house, while Abby and Lloyd followed him, walking hand in hand. Her parents were inside cleaning up after breakfast. When they entered their house, Klem went over to Lloyd while saying, "There you are, my boy! Abby said you already ate, so have a seat."

Lloyd obliged his offer and took a place on the couch. He reminded himself that he had better keep track of the time. Lloyd liked to converse with Klem. Many times, Lloyd would seek him out at the lighthouse. They would talk about world events, our *nation*, and of course, God's seaside creation. Sometimes the two of them would share their lunch break, talking between munches of their sandwiches. This morning, Klem wanted to describe some things from his latest delivery of souvenir items for the lighthouse gift store.

After about fifteen minutes, Abby cruised into the living room and sat on the couch, next to Lloyd. With both hands, she was tapping lightly on the top of each knees in kind of a nervous way. Finally, she could not wait any longer and turned to Lloyd and asked, "So what did you get me for my birthday, big guy? You didn't forget this very important date, did you?"

"Of course not, honey, and I have it right here."

He took out a gift card from his pocket and handed it to her.

"I hope you don't mind. I didn't get you a birthday card, but I can have one to give you when I come back tonight for cake and ice cream."

Hearing Lloyd's voice, Parker started in again with his little singing about birthday cake and ice cream. Abby took the gift card and carefully opened it. After she read its message, she exclaimed, "Oh my God! Oh my dear God in heaven! You gave me the best present I could ever receive! You gave me three whole hours to sail on a Sunfish! Oh my gosh!"

She took another close look and saw that it was scheduled for a half hour from now. Jumping up from the couch, she said, "I have to get ready! And I want everyone else to come too! I want you to see me sail! Oh, Lloyd, this is just fantastic! I am so excited!"

Abby ran upstairs to gather her things, at the same time Jane came from the kitchen. Looking at the boys, she asked, "What in the world was all that yelling? Is everyone okay in here?"

Lloyd felt that he needed to apologize to Jane since Abby received her present from him without her being there to watch.

"I am sorry that she got her birthday present already, but Abby almost grabbed it from my hands."

"Oh, that is perfectly fine. No need to apologize, but what in our dear God's creation did you give my daughter?"

Just then, Abby came running down the steps, two at a time.

"Mom, I am going sailing, and please, please come and watch!"

Jane untied her apron and said, "Of course I will watch. You have talked about sailing forever, but none of us have actually seen you do your stuff!"

The boys stood up from their places and walked over to the closet to get jackets. Klem reached up to the upper shelf and brought down his binoculars so they could take them. He handed them to Parker and then took his car keys from the hook by the front door.

They all headed to the car. In short time, with Klem at the wheel, they were traveling to the inlet. Parker was singing in the back seat, and Abby was next to him, smiling and holding her gift card tightly in her hands. Jane and Lloyd shared the front seat alongside Klem. After almost no time, they were pulling into the small parking lot of *Big Duck Inlet Sailing Rentals.* Abby was the first person out of the car with her gift card being held tightly in her hand.

The rental place was tucked away on the east side of the inlet. It was not much more than an oversized shed with a wraparound wooden plank porch. Dry-docked on the porch were four Sunfish boats and one Aero. As soon as Abby walked up to the shed, Linda came out to meet them.

"You must be Abby, the accomplished sailor that your friend told me about over the phone. I have your Sunfish all cleaned up and ready for you."

She lightly pushed on the back of the first Sunfish, sliding it onto the sand, a few feet from the water.

"Okay, Abby, it is all yours, but first, please put on the life jacket that is in the hull. It is a medium size, so it should fit you."

Abby slipped on her jacket and zipped it up in the front. She had smiles from head to foot.

"Mom, could you please take my picture using my cellphone?"

She posed for a second, then moved the boat farther into the shallow water. Linda immediately saw that she did not have to help her customer. Abby slipped her legs into the smooth molded hull, sitting with her legs stretched out straight. She checked the tightness of the sail and moved the boom back and forth a few times. Abby navigated her sailboat with professional ease as she went deeper into the bay.

The wind started to fill the sail as it came from the west. It gave her a delight as well as a total thrill. She pushed down on the rod to fully plunge the center board into the water and instinctively started to heel, by leaning over to the side for balance and control.

Her spectators left the rental store and found a long bench at the shoreline that was big enough for all of them to watch. From time to time, each stood holding binoculars up to their eyes to get a closer look. Jane passed the field glasses to Parker for his turn. After focusing the eyepieces, he exclaimed, "I can see Mom, and she is smiling!"

Klem said, "Let's all wave and see if she can wave back. Abby looks pretty busy way out there, but maybe she will see us."

They all started to wave at once, and after almost a full minute, she returned their wave with one of her own.

Starting the second hour, the wind picked up, and the spectators could see that the Sunfish was beautifully cutting through the water with ease. Abby was fully enjoying every minute, performing various maneuvers to make graceful directional changes for the fun of it. She was totally enthralled with her ability to remember how to fully command her Sunfish. While slicing through the waves, she had flickers of college memories with her and Terri enjoying their sailing together.

The minutes melted away into another hour, then three hours, amounting to the time limit for her. Abby carefully maneuvered her Sunfish once again to the beach in front of the rental shed. She was greeted with a standing applause from her family. While pulling off her life jacket, Lloyd handed a towel for her to dry off. She eagerly took it and quickly wrapped herself with the towel having only her face showing.

"Oh, that was so terrific! I loved every minute! Thank you, Lloyd!"

Heading back to the car, Klem thought that Abby would feel cold very soon, if she wasn't already. He hurried ahead of them and, once inside, warmed up the car by dialing up the temperature and putting the fan on maximum.

They all piled in, Parker on one side of his mom and Lloyd on the other. Being so proud of his mom, he said, "Mom, you were great! I did not know that you were so good at sailing!"

CHAPTER
11

Dinner and Another Community Meeting

In Port James, Maine, people say that their weeks moved along so quickly. Some remarked that being busy seemed to make this happen. With Maine's short growing season, gardening around people's homes had to be performed quickly. As soon as June arrived, the topsoil had to be prepared for the plants and flowers. Fertilizing was always necessary as well as watering. Of course, these tasks had to be fitted around and between the forty-hour workweeks.

So the next community meeting of the summer was to convene once again at the village hall on Tuesday. For that particular evening, Klem was not home yet from working at the Port James lighthouse. Jane could not remember if she had mentioned to Klem that they had asked Lloyd over for dinner. She had extended this invitation so that she, hubby, Abby, Parker along with Lloyd could walk over to the meeting all together.

Just then, Klem came in through the back door and entered the kitchen. He took off his lightweight jacket and hung it up on a wooden hook just inside from the door. Closing it behind him, he eyed Jane fixing the plate settings at the table. As soon as she had her last plate located, Klem surprised her by giving her a hug from the back. Jane smiled and said, "Well, that sure feels good, and you had better be my husband!"

Thinking quickly, Klem responded, "Well, I definitely know *who I am*, but I certainly hope *you* are my wife!"

Jane rolled her eyes and turned around.

"Oh, hi, Klem, darling. How was your day? Are the rose hips around the lighthouse starting to bud yet? By the way, tonight is the community meeting, and Lloyd is coming over for dinner."

Klem walked over to the paper calendar that hung on the side of the refrigerator. Even with smartphones, the Watercrests still used their calendar to keep themselves on schedule. It literally contained their whole life activities. Jane would never throw out the previous calendars because they served as their collective diaries. Occasionally, she needed to dig through them to see whose turn it was to host Thanksgiving, Christmas, birthdays, or any other get-togethers. Klem lifted several pages to see a few more months, then turned around and asked, "What's for dinner?"

Just then, Lloyd knocked on the screen door a few times and came in from the front porch.

Greeting them both, he said, "How's my favorite couple doing today? Gosh, Jane, something smells wonderful! By any chance, could it be your world-famous Yankee pot roast?"

Jane received his compliment by twirling her wooden spoon with a flourish over her head followed by making a deep curtsy. Hearing Lloyd's knock on the door, Parker skipped downstairs and ran up to Lloyd for a hug. Abby came a few minutes later and went to him for a kiss. After their greetings, they all paraded into the kitchen.

When they all sat down to eat, Jane led them in a word of prayer.

"Dear heavenly Father, thank You for this evening and our food that comes from Your hand. For those who are not as fortunate as us, please help them have enough to nourish their bodies. Thank You for the love that is shared among us. We ask that You help Parker's body as he fights his infection. Amen."

After everyone had seconds followed by Jane's homemade chocolate cookies, Klem helped her to clean up the kitchen and load the dishwasher. Within twenty minutes, they were heading out into the cool night air on their way to the village hall. This time, Parker was allowed to come with them since he had an extra-long nap after lunch.

As they walked along, Parker placed himself with Abby on the right and Lloyd on the left. He was holding their hands, and every once in a while, they lifted Parker's legs off the sidewalk so he could swing a few times. "Wee! Wee!" he exclaimed as they swung him to-and-fro.

Rounding the last block, they arrived at the village hall steps and entered the meeting room. The five of them quickly found their chairs and waited for Sarah while having congenial conversations with friends sitting near them.

Promptly at seven o'clock, Sarah walked up to the podium. She organized her agenda papers and asked to convene by having those in attendance stand for the Pledge of Allegiance.

"Good evening, everyone, thank you for coming tonight. Please sign the attendance sheet on the clipboard as it is passed around. Now, let's see…the first item relates to the fundraiser to purchase items in the lighthouse gift store.

"As most of you know, Caroline is Klem Watercrest's volunteer assistant for the Port James lighthouse gift store. A few days ago, she was nice enough to make a wish list of what they are hoping to purchase. Some of the items that they would like to stock on their shelves are nautical key chains, lighthouse picture books, lobster floats, lighthouse postcards, sweatshirts, and hats, lighthouse patches and Port James decals.

"So let me describe this fundraiser that I have on the agenda. It is the annual event and fundraiser at our lighthouse. It will be one of those world-famous lobster feasts. I know all of you here tonight, and all our nice out-of-towners, love this tasty event. By the way, it has raised quite a few thousand dollars in the past. This year, advanced tickets will be sold by Arnold over there in the back row.

"I believe everyone knows Arnold, but for those that do not, could you stand up so we can all see you?"

Arnold stood up, and the attendees turned around in their chairs to see him standing. After a few moments, he sat back down, and Sarah continued, "Thank you, Arnold, and by the way, thanks for coordinating the ticket sales. I will start a sign-up sheet for those who may want to volunteer for any number of jobs to make this festival once again a great success. It certainly *will be* a success, and I am looking forward to attending. Oh, for those that don't know, Pastor Tucker, the pastor of the Congregational Church in town, said that their membership will help host this event.

"The church's huge kitchen will be used to steam the lobsters and cook the corn and salt potatoes. For me, it is always fun to pop into their church kitchen and see Pastor Tucker. He wears a striped shirt under an apron instead of his black-and-white clericals. His shirt sleeves are rolled up past his elbows, but…I regress. Now where was I? Oh yes. Their courtyard, which has a nice view of our lighthouse, will be set up with tables and chairs for eating."

Sarah had a twinkle in the eyes and said, "Not for eating the *tables and chairs*, but for eating *their meals*. Ha! Ha! Hmm…I will continue. I think the courtyard is large enough to seat a little more than sixty guests. The parishioners also secure one of those huge white party tents…just in case there is unfavorable weather on festival day."

Sarah walked around the podium and handed the volunteer sign-up sheet and clipboard to the first attendee in the front row. Stepping back to the podium, she reached on the top shelf and took a sip of water. Then she spoke again, "As we all know, Port James is a proud community. We are also *community minded*—that is, whenever possible, our residents shop locally. Our businesses have been here such a long time. Some go back over one hundred years, having three or more generations working at the same, family-owned shops. No big box boxes in Port James, thank goodness!

"So, to promote our businesses, we have asked each store owner to make a nautical sculpture outside on their sidewalk. Well, we have had a terrific response. I'm sure you all have admired these sculptures as you walk and shop in our village. For those that may not have had the pleasure, let me think of some. Hank from the gasoline station made a sailboat out of plywood, Beth from her bakery made a huge conch shell, Bert from the hardware store created a beautiful replica of Port James lighthouse. The Walkers from Walker's Market made

a statue of a sea captain dressed in full uniform. It is so realistic...
which leads me to the final piece of artwork that is also so realistic.

"It is at the eyeglass store of Jerome Floss. Mr. Floss is not here
tonight. Is that right?"

Sarah took off her reading glasses and glanced around the room
to see if he was present. Being assured that he did not come, she
said, "In Mr. Floss's absence, I will try to describe his piece of work.
Well...it is a mermaid that...hmm...well let me put it this way, is...
anatomically correct...on the top. Now it truly is nice and all, but
need it be so realistic especially on the upper half? Who wants to
talk to Jerome about gluing two seashells on the...hmm...shall I say,
well-endowed mermaid? Anyone?

"Let me add that it has slowed down traffic, especially from
vacationers who are looking for a place to park. Do I see any hands
for a volunteer to nicely talk to Jerome? No? Okay...I guess that it
will have to be me. Maybe I will offer two large seashells from my
own shell collection, that would be nice."

A few of the menfolk thought to themselves, while others whispered under their breath, "I like it the way it is."

"Now if no one has anything else to bring to this meeting, I have one last item."

Clearing her throat for comfort and to buy some time to collect herself, Sarah placed both hands on her podium, looked around the meeting room a few seconds, and continued, "It seems that Louise Parson needed a ride to her doctor's office last week. After a few phone calls, she got Gertrude Baker to give her a ride. Well, as you know, doctor's appointments can take a long time, most of it spent sitting in the waiting room. As the story goes, Gertrude left Louise off and decided to drive to the creamery store for a double scoop of chocolate peanut butter swirl ice cream in a cone. No, I think it was in a dish…well, that doesn't matter. What matters is that Gertrude, the poor dear, completely and innocently, forgot Louise at her doctor's and went straight home. It was only after her pleasant two-hour afternoon nap that she woke straight up in bed and remembered Louise.

"By that time however…now, friends, this is really true. Pitiful Louise saw that Gertrude's green car was not in the parking lot, so she took matters into her own hands. To get a ride home, she hiked up her long skirt, showed some legs… right on our Main Street!

"All this is to say that Port James could use a *Helping Neighbors Organization* that would have the names and telephone numbers of some younger folk who would be willing to drive our senior residents."

As luck would have it, to help people like Louise, several younger residents raised their hands to be on the *Helping Neighbors* list.

Relieved that she got through this spicy community meeting, Sarah took a deep cleansing breath and offered up a prayer to close the meeting.

12

Sharing Something and a Prayer

It was midday at Port James and getting quite a bit warmer as the summer progressed. The day before, Abby had asked Lloyd if they could go to the cliff where Klem's lighthouse was located near the water's edge. For some reason, she wanted to meet him there, instead of walking together.

Abby took the footpath from her home to the light and arrived there at a little past noon. She saw Klem was using a cloth to wipe down the collected dust from the white park bench a few steps from the base of the lighthouse. As he inspected his work, he noticed that a few of the wooden slats were starting to wear out, presenting some small surface slivers.

"Hi, Dad, it sure looks like we are in for some sunny weather for the next few days. Your rose hips sure are doing fine this year."

Klem stood up and placed his hands on his back to work out a little kink.

"Hi, my daughter! Yes, those flower bushes certainly like the salt air and sunshine. As you know, I always have to prune them back a little. Otherwise, they will take over the whole place. I have made good use of those thick working gloves you gave me for Christmas. So far, I have not gotten any thorns stuck in my skin. So...did you come to see me, or are you just taking a walk today to enjoy God's creation?"

"I'm going to meet Lloyd here in a few. In fact, I think I see him coming up from the path right now. I am hoping that he will climb to the top of your lighthouse with me."

"Well now, Abby, why wouldn't he want to?"

Klem looked back down the path and could see Lloyd approaching them a little distance away.

"Abby, sure enough, as we speak, I see your man taking the last turn in the path right now, and he looks happy to see you."

Lloyd was wearing carpenter's pants with outside pockets on each side. He had a long-sleeve white summer-weight shirt, which showed his nice chest muscles underneath the smooth and refined material. He looked like a male model from an L.L.Bean catalog. His brilliant smile seemed to make the sun follow him, glowing beautifully around him. Abby felt her heartbeat quicken for his masculine perfection, but also for what she needed to tell him. Feeling a little shaky, she stood there and waited for his warm hug and kiss. He paused in his steps just before embracing Abby and then turned to greet Klem.

"Hi, Klem, how are you today? I noticed that you were looking at the condition of your bench. I can cut a few new slats to replace some of those old ones if you would like. Suppose I will bring them over later in the week."

Abby interrupted his offer by extending her arms outward in his direction to get her hug. Klem decided to keep in the background, so he quickly thanked Lloyd for the nice offer and headed toward the lighthouse gift shop.

Abby and Lloyd went hand in hand to the edge of the cliff to look at the breakers rolling into the beach. A number of the stronger waves reached the serrated rocks wetting them with a salt spray before retreating back to the depths. As the two remained standing there, they breathed in the fresh salt air and felt the warm sunshine on their faces. Abby was the first to speak.

"Lloyd, will you come up to the top of the lighthouse with me? I feel a real need to share something important with you."

Lloyd had no idea what she needed to tell him. In silence, they both turned toward the lighthouse and entered through the iron door. As they climbed the spiral metal staircase, she smiled a few times, but there was no conversation between them. As they went up, Abby's hand brushed against the cool, dark stone walls. It gave her a shiver as she thought that *cool and dark* may soon be Lloyd's feeling toward her.

When they reached the top, the windows were clean and clear. There was a noticeable light odor of window cleaning spray that Klem had just used for his morning routine an hour before. Abby turned to Lloyd and asked, "Lloyd, let's go onto the outside deck, if that is okay with you. And...please give me a few minutes to compose myself."

They both stood very close to each other but did not speak. Off in the distance, it looked like the sunshine may soon give way to some developing storm clouds. Finally, Abby spoke, "Lloyd dearest, a while back, I received a letter that I need to respond to. The person who sent this letter and I have had an agreement for over four years. Now please understand that I have a possible life-changing decision to make rather shortly.

She tenderly released her right hand from his and reached a finger up to his lips.

"Before you say anything, let me assure you that I will always love us. *Always.*"

Lloyd believed her assurance, but it did not seem enough to fill his instant emptiness. He could not believe that she was struggling with something like this within her soul. His strong legs felt like they were holding up a ton of anxiety. He searched her blue eyes for any clue to help him understand, but there was none.

"You just have to believe me, Lloyd, that you will be the first to know when things happen. Do you believe me?"

For the very first time in their relationship, Lloyd said, "Abby, you need to know...I am fully and totally in love with you."

"And, Lloyd, my dearest man, I have fallen deeply in love with you too. I thank God every day for your love, both for me and for my son, Parker. Now could I ask you to do something for us before we go back down? Would you hold my hands even tighter and pray with me?"

Lloyd nodded and said, "Of course."

Abby closed her eyes and felt the strong attraction between them, but also her solid bond with her divine Creator.

"Dear heavenly Father, God Almighty, thank You for my new founded love for Lloyd. True love is Your gift to us mortals here on Your earth. Again, I deeply thank You with all my being. We are told that You already know our inner thoughts, but You want to hear our prayers. Please help me as I work through a huge decision in my life. I ask for You to be with me...I ask for Your guiding hand always but especially in the next few weeks. Please love and help Lloyd understand my love for him, and help him accept anything that may happen in our future. Give us both strength and courage, and help us to do what you would want us to do in our lives. You are a good God, and I love You, and in all ways, may Your will be done. Amen."

Now that Abby's prayer request was received in God's heavenly kingdom, she looked into her man's eyes and said, "Remember, Lloyd, I will always love you."

Then they opened the door, went inside, and started the downward climb.

As Lloyd took one step at a time, his spirit was feeling a little more uplifted after Abby assured him that she truly loved him so very much. In fact, even though she still had not shared the exact details of her dilemma as yet, he felt even closer to her. She was so sincere, not like so many other women, and above all, he really felt the love she had for him.

CHAPTER 13

Breakfast and Making Some Time

Two days ago, after returning from the community meeting, Lloyd promised to Parker that they would do something together on Saturday. When Abby heard them talking, she said that even though she wished to join them for the *boys' day out*, she would be writing cover letters and filling out job applications for journalism positions.

On the night before, Parker had a little more trouble getting to sleep. He wondered what they would be doing together. After his bedtime prayers, he thought, *Maybe we are going to do something with those seashells that we found when we went beach combing. Or maybe just a nice walk or a visit at the piers to look at the boats. Maybe...*

Then feeling the day's activities catching up to him, he fell asleep. Just liked Lloyd promised, the next morning, he arrived at the Watercrest's door. Abby already had her coffee, and Jane was frying eggs, sunny-side-up, while Klem was in charge of the toast. He liked all his food warmer than most, so he had stacked five plates and placed them in the microwave for about ninety seconds. When the microwave bell rang, he said, "Well, that should have heated those plates up enough to keep my toast warm throughout breakfast."

Jane looked at her contented man, the love of her life. He was currently rather pleased with himself. She replied, "Yes, Klem dear. The first time you did that, I thought you were a little crazy. But now, I have seen the light. Speaking of seeing things, could you let Lloyd in? He is coming up to the front door."

They both smiled whenever Lloyd was with them. This day, they had even more affection knowing that Parker and he would be sharing part of the day together.

Lloyd and Klem walked into the kitchen together as Abby and Parker came downstairs. Klem said, "Well guess who I found at our front door just now? It was Lloyd! But for you English majors who might be present, that was not a real question. It was merely a rhetorical one. Now...the word *rhetorical* comes from the Latin root word *rheto* from where we get the word rhinoceros, meaning hmm... ugh...hmm."

Parker was rubbing his eyes from sleep but managed to give a guess. "Grandpa, does it mean stubborn?"

"Why yes, that is right, my little man in the front row, exactly. So the answer to my question that I presented to this audience is *stubborn*. In laymen's terms, my question is not really looking for an answer. It stands on its own."

Parker said, "I get it! Yes! Just like a rhetorical question! It is not looking for an answer. It stands there just like a rhinoceros! Right, Grandpa?"

Jane changed her gaze from looking at her eggs and looked at her husband. Rolling her eyes, she said, "Now, Klem, shame on you! If you keep filling Parker's head with silly stuff, he will have to go to special classes to unlearn your totally made-up facts!"

Parker looked on and listened to his grandparent's conservation that was happening between them in the kitchen.

"Oh, Grandma, I know when Grandpa is just being funny. Just like the other day when it was sunny out. Grandpa said for me to go outside and close my eyes."

Jane turned back around to monitor the cooking. Over her right shoulder, she asked, "Now why did he want you to do that?"

"He said that when I close my eyes, it becomes an eclipse of the sun! And, Grandma, it worked!"

Jane walked from the stove and placed two eggs on the pre-heated plates, which were on the kitchen counter. She then said,

"Klem, please take the plates over to the table. And by the way, Klem, see what I mean? That poor grandson of ours will be twenty years old and still in grade school!"

Jane sat down, and smiling at everyone, she folded her hands in prayer.

"Thank You God for this food…and for common sense. Amen."

* * * * *

It wasn't long before Klem, Parker, and Lloyd started their little walk up the path to the lighthouse. Klem parted from them as he unlocked the door to the gift house. He had to jiggle the doorknob lock up and down a few times before he could get in. Once that was accomplished, he said, "You men have a good time today. Let me know if you discover anything new that the world needs to know."

He watched the boys walk around the other side of the lighthouse. When they were out of sight, he went into the gift store and turned on the lights. From the previous day, Klem had left some items that were still in their Amazon Prime delivery box. Since they still needed to be placed on the shelves, he decided that it would be his first job to accomplish.

Meanwhile, outside on the lighthouse lawn, Parker and Lloyd were examining the shells they had strategically and carefully arranged on the ground the day before. Having Parker's full attention, Lloyd was explaining something to him as he pointed to the shells.

"Parker, remember that yesterday, every hour, we placed a seashell on the lighthouse shadow. As the sun travels across the sky, the lighthouse shadow touches each seashell, one at a time. You had placed the first shell on the lawn at nine o'clock in the morning. Now, I see by my watch that it is just ten o'clock. Where is the shadow now?"

Parker walked closer to the shell and said, "I see that it is just touching the second shell. Hey, Lloyd! The shadow was on the first shell at nine o'clock, and now since it is on the second shell, it must be ten o'clock! I get it, Lloyd, when the lighthouse shadow is halfway to the third shell, it will be ten-thirty! Wow!"

"Right you are, Parker! With six simple shells, we have built a clock!"

Parker could not wait any longer; he just had to show his grandpa. Running across the lawn and up to the gift store steps, he opened the door and ran inside.

"Grandpa! Grandpa! You have to see the clock Lloyd and I made outside."

Klem was quite perplexed at Parker's statement. He placed his scenic gift plates on the shelf that were next to some small lighthouse souvenirs. With Parker reaching for his hand, they both went through the gift store and down the outside steps. Still holding his hand and pulling a little, Klem was taken to the other side of the lighthouse. Parker stopped, looked up at Klem, and said, "See? See, Grandpa? We made a clock out of seashells!"

Klem checked his shirt pocket and found his eyeglasses. Placing them on, he carefully walked around the display several times.

"Well, gentlemen, I plumb believe that you have made a mighty fine sundial! This is the best sundial I ever have seen in my entire life! Looking at the shadow and the seashells, I believe it is a few minutes past ten o'clock. Is that right?"

Parker was just beaming with delight, and so was Lloyd. The three of them stayed there a while, admiring both the beautiful day and the sundial.

"Now, boys, I need to get back to the gift store, but at twelve o'clock, I will have my lunch. Now, all I have to do is look outside my side window at your sundial and see if it is noontime. Thanks, boys!"

Looking up at Lloyd, Parker declared, "This is the best day of my life!"

CHAPTER
14

Kicking Down the Road

After making the largest sundial in all of Port James, Parker and Lloyd left the lighthouse grounds and headed back down the gravel and sand footpath. The little trail went past the Watercrest's home before leading onto the village sidewalk. Parker held Lloyd's hand out of admiration and love for his grown-up buddy. Walking past their house, Parker looked up at Lloyd and asked, "Later on today, when my mom and grandma have the time, can we show them the clock we made? I know Mom is sending out some letters for a job and my grandma is doing the laundry. I can smell the clean sheets blowing in the ocean breeze. I kind of like that fresh smell. It kind of reminds me of...hmm...family. Lloyd, do you like that smell too?"

"Well, yes, it is a pleasant smell. It reminds me of my own mother. When I was your age, I think it gave me a feeling of security and love, if that makes any sense."

Parker said, "Sure, it makes sense, Lloyd." *It is your feelings.*

They made it to the end of the path and then stepped up onto the village sidewalk. As they strolled along, Parker made it a game as he stepped over the sidewalk cracks. A block away was one of Port James's oldest evergreen trees. The trunk was almost two feet across at the base. It had showered the sidewalk with pine cones, which delighted Parker. He spied the largest one and kicked it as far as he could, about five feet in front of them.

"Now it's your turn, Dad, I mean Lloyd! How far can you kick it down the sidewalk?"

Lloyd stepped up to it and made his best effort. Then Parker followed. This little exchange between friends cost nothing, but in some ways, it was priceless. Finally, the cone found a storm sewer and disappeared below the grate.

By this time, they had gone into a section of Port James that had homes boasting of varied architecture. Lloyd used this opportunity to point out some styles.

"Parker, see that house across the street? That is Beth's home. She has her own bakery in town. She makes the best blueberry turnovers you ever tasted. That house was built in the Queen Ann style. See the attached gazebo on the left side…like the ones I build? That home also has some fish scale shingles up at the center gable peak. See those shingles? They really do look like fish scales."

"Yea, Lloyd, I see them, and they really look like the sides of fish. Can you tell me about that next house across the street on our left?"

"Sure, that one is a bungalow. They are usually a one-story home, having a small second story with a dormer. The dormer gives the second floor a little more room. Because the house is on the smaller side, bungalows have large, deep porches to make up for the size."

"Hmm…that makes sense. How about this huge one we are going by now?"

"That is owned by the manager of Port James Credit Union. A credit union is similar to a bank, Parker. Now, that is a perfect example of the Georgian style. The first Georgian building was built in the year 1695. It was located at the College of William and Mary in Williamsburg, Virginia. They called it the Wren building. As you can see, Parker, it is a full two-story home. Above the two floors, you can see that they have an enormous attic. Parker, how many windows are there on each floor? Can you count them?"

After the boys were walking a short while, Parker stopped. Using his finger, he pointed at each window and counted.

"One, two, three…let's see, there are three on one side of the front door and three on the other side. There are seven on the second floor and then five above that. Wow, that house has eighteen windows just in the front!"

Lloyd was thrilled that little Parker was so interested in learning the different kinds of architectures. When he designed and built gazebos, porches, and even decks and sheds, he kept his designs accurate and close to the same style to match the homeowner's dwelling.

"Say, Parker, we are only a few blocks away from the gazebo that I am currently working on. So far, it is only the deck, but would you like to see it?"

"Wow, would I love that!"

When the duo arrived at the next block, they turned left. By the time they went three more blocks, they ended at the water's edge, called *Big Duck Inlet*.

"So what do you think, Parker? How does it look to you so far?"

Parker just stood there in complete amazement. Then came the pile of questions.

"Man oh man! Did you do this all by yourself? How much wood did you use? How will you get all the way to the top? How *will you make the top?* Are you going to put fish scale shingles on the roof? I think that would look cool. Will there be windows like the ones on that banker's house that we walked by?"

"Parker, my friend, would you like to sit up here on the gazebo deck?"

Without waiting, he took Parker by the waist and lifted him carefully up onto the deck floor. He then joined Parker by placing his own hands on the deck and pushed himself up next to his buddy. With crossed legs, the two of them looked at the beautiful bay. Far in the distance, a lobster boat was just appearing. It looked like a small toy as it headed to the bay.

Much closer to them, they watched the sandpipers make like a chorus line of dancers along the sand to dig for shrimp. On the beach was a vestige of a sandcastle that someone had made earlier on. The little but constant bay tide waves repeatedly lapped over the structure. Parker looked at Lloyd and remarked, "I guess nothing is permanent, is it?" Lloyd nodded. "But how about your gazebos? Are they permanent forever and ever?"

"Let me put it this way, Parker. When I build something, my customers pay me with their hard-earned money. They expect that I will do my best quality of work. I tell them the truth. Nothing is forever, but I build everything to last seventy or even more years. They like that truthful answer, and many times, they hire me."

Parker smiled, then from their vantage point, looked far out to the horizon, and said, "My Sunday school teacher says nothing is forever except Jesus's love for us."

Looking over to their far right was a boat pier and dock with a little lobster shack, they watched the action unfold as the captain of the lobster boat eased the laden vessel near the pier. Like actors in a well-rehearsed play, two deckhands jumped onto the pier to tie off their boat. For the next half hour, Lloyd and Parker saw them take containers that held their catch from the boat. On the deck, the crew quickly organized the lobster by size. A man from the shack came out to help the crew. With the exchange of papers, and after some communication with each other, the lobster boat was untied and left for another fishing excursion.

Although completely entertained, Parker went back to his previous questions for Lloyd. "So could you tell me about building this gazebo of yours?"

"Okay, my friend, let me see. To hold up the gazebo deck, I use pressure-treated posts about this big. They will have to hold up the weight of the entire gazebo."

Lloyd showed how large around they were by holding his hands six inches from each other. Right next to where they were sitting, Lloyd had a few plans in a plastic folder. He shuffled through them until he found the post plans. Handing the paper to Parker, he explained a few details.

"I call this sketch *post plans.* I use this plan for all of my gazebos that I construct."

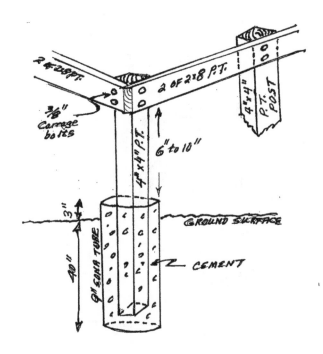

"I have to dig holes for each post that is about seventy inches deep. This is so the winter frost will not lift them partly out of the ground. Now, Parker, most of the time, the soil is not even that deep before I hit what is known as bedrock. So when that happens, I don't have to dig any farther. I also use these same posts for the railing verticals."

Lloyd was concerned that Parker would be getting bored, but it didn't look like it. In fact, he re-asked one of his original questions.

"How, for crying in a fish bait bucket, do you get way up there in the air to make the roof?"

"Hmm…well I think it would be easier if I show you another illustration that I drew. Let's see, I think I have it. Ah yes, here it is. This plan is called *scaffolding plan.*"

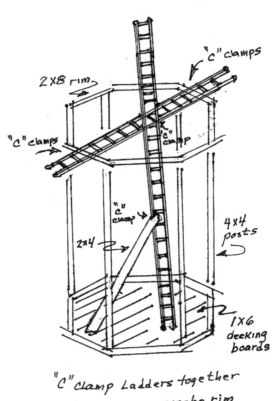

"C" Clamp Ladders together
and onto upper gazebo rim
"C" clamp 2x4 to Ladder

"See? I use what is called C clamps to hold boards to the eight-sided roof rim. The same kind of clamps also hold the ladder to the boards. Even though I do not like heights, and I really mean, *do not*, when I make this original kind of scaffolding, I can easily and safely climb that high. When I do not need the scaffolding anymore, I can easily unscrew the C clamps and use the wood for something else."

"Wow, Lloyd! That is really cool. How about the roof? What kind of shingles are you going to use?"

"Well, I give the owner several shapes and colors of shingles to choose from. The owners really liked the shingles that are called tab shingles. Parker, you are going to like this. When I finish the roof, the entire roof will look like fish scales, how about that?"

Parker smiled and put his six-year-old imagination to work. He closed his eyes and said, "I think the shingles will look like a mermaid's tail."

With more smiles, Lloyd then decided that it was past lunchtime. He thought about where to go and said to Parker, "Let's follow our noses back toward home and get some lunch!"

Lloyd lifted Parker from his seating spot on the gazebo deck; then, he jumped down to the ground and next to him. Strolling on the sidewalk, they retraced their steps until Parker ran ahead to climb up onto an old cement block to stand on it. The block had survived being there between the sidewalk and the edge of the street for over one hundred years. Within a few seconds, Lloyd had also arrived at the block. With his hand, Lloyd felt the rough texture of the cement surface. Then Parker went into a seating position.

"Lloyd, why do you think that they made this block in the first place?

Lloyd helped him off the century-old cement and back onto the sidewalk. He replied, "Before the invention of cars, the residents of Port James had horse and buggies to take them places. The buggy door where the passengers came out from was about three feet above the street. So, this was like a step that they could use to get onto the sidewalk. Also, see that black iron post that has a ring going through it?"

Parker looked at the black post and then went up to the cast iron ring and moved with his hand back and forth a few times.

"That black iron ring was used to tie or hitch up the horse reins so their horses would not stroll away."

"Sometimes my mom says that I should have horse reins so that I don't run off when we are going someplace."

Lloyd tried to imagine how that would be beneficial but then decided that it would be rather odd. They walked along and toward the business section of Port James. Parker was skipping ahead and humming a song he learned in school. Sometimes he made a running jump to catch a few leaves from a low-hanging tree branch. It made Lloyd's heart sing to see this little boy being so happy.

As Lloyd watched him run ahead, he recounted Parker's little life so far. At the age of four, he lost his father in the fishing accident; then two years later, his mother brought him to social services and left him. After all that happening in his little life, he comes down with Lyme disease.

After passing Barton's Hardware store and Walker's Market, they came up to Beth's Bakery. The boys cupped their hands around their faces as they peered through the large glass windows. They could see Beth and her daughter, Nichole, helping customers pick out a pound or two of cookies that were arranged in the glass display cabinets.

"Parker, let's go inside. I have an idea."

With Parker just behind, they swung open the bakery door and were greeted with the rich, sweet aroma of Italian cookies, cakes, and fresh bread. Before the little bell on the door stopped jingling, Beth looked up and asked, "Hello, Lloyd! Look here! Just who do you have with you today?"

Parker stepped up and announced, with pride in his voice, "I am Parker, Lloyd's very best friend…that is right along with my mom. Do you know my mom? Her name is Abby, and she is very pretty!"

By this time, Nichole dusted off flour from her white canvas apron and walked up to join the three. With a little humor, she said, "I hope you two are staying out of trouble on this fine day!"

This was Parker's invitation to chime in.

"We have been on a walk, and I saw a gazebo that Lloyd is building over at Big Duck Inlet. It's real cool, and I sure learned a lot today! Do you know that the style of your house is Queen Ann?"

Beth looked at Nichole, then back at Parker. "Well, now, I did not know that. I will have to tell my husband."

While they conversed, Lloyd was reading a small menu that listed some premade sandwiches.

"Say, Beth, us guys have worked up a pretty large appetite. Do you still have some of these sandwiches left?"

"Oh, let's see. Nichole, are there still some left in that refrigerator case?"

In Nichole's life, she was planning her wedding to her heart-throb named Patrick. As she walked over to the fridge, she thought how wonderful it would be to have a little boy like Parker. She opened the refrigerator door and looked inside.

"It appears that we have tuna salad on whole wheat and..."

Parker didn't let her continue any further, and with excitement, he said, "Sold! I love tuna!"

In the corner of the bakery, there was one little roundtable and two wire chairs for them to eat their lunch. Lloyd pulled the tall wire chair away from the table, then lifted Parker up to the seat. He pushed Parker snuggly up to the table. Nichole brought them the sandwiches and their milks. After wolfing down their sandwiches, Lloyd got Beth's attention.

"Excuse me, Beth, but do you think we can have two of your wonderful blueberry turnovers? They would hit the spot, along with a little more milk."

Beth brought over the turnovers, one for each plate. Parker looked at his plate then at Lloyd and asked, "Lloyd, should I have a knife and fork to eat this, or should I just pick it up with my hands?"

"Well, Parker, you could eat it either way, but I just use my hands, but be careful, sometimes the blueberries can squirt out the ends. So I usually eat it over the plate so I can scoop up the drippings if that happens."

Parker did not take a long time to dig into his after-meal treat... using his hands.

Pausing between munches of his heavenly dessert, Parker said to his friend something that just about melted Lloyd's heart whenever he hears Parker say it.

"Lloyd, this has been the best day of my life!"

CHAPTER 15

Now Is the Time to Tell

The upstairs bedroom that was Abby's since birth had six glass panes, which perfectly framed the Port James lighthouse. This morning, like countless previous ones, Abby opened her eyes from her night's sleep and, while still in her bed, gazed out this same window. She reminisced that as a child, how this lighthouse view helped her to guess what kind of weather was occurring outside.

If the lighthouse windows at the top were cloudy and wet, then it probably rained over the night. A cleaner look to the lighthouse's exterior meant a sunny day was in store for her to play outside with her little friends. It was quite obvious to her that the lighthouse was warning of a cold winter day whenever the sight of white snow was swirling around its base. But on those enchanting days when the air was heavy with fog, she didn't have to sit upright to look out. From under the sheets, little Abby could hear the melodic sound of its fog horn "talking" to the vessels still at sea. Somehow its repetitious song was reassuring to her. It had strength and predictability that felt soothing, almost like her mother's touch on her forehead when she didn't feel very well.

So this morning as Abby laid in bed, she once again wondered what scene was outside her window. Sitting up in bed for a closer look, she saw that indeed there was a fog in the air, but it had already started to wane. She felt that it paralleled what she needed to talk about to Lloyd. Maybe it would clear the air between them, so to speak.

Twisting around to slide out of her warm sheets, she placed her feet on the floor, then tapped around with her toes to find her slippers. With that maneuver completed, she quietly found her bedroom door and opened it to the hallway. Walking down the hall, she paused to check on Parker. She opened his door to peek inside. Seeing that he was still sleeping soundly, she closed it again and went down the stairs and into the kitchen.

Klem was already waiting for his blend of New England vanilla coffee to perk through the Keurig and into his mug.

"Good morning, my little lovely. How did you sleep? Do you want me to put in a K cup for you?"

"Good morning, Dad. Thanks! That would be perfect. I am going to meet Lloyd outside on the front porch this morning. I called him last night, and he agreed to be here in a few minutes, that is, if it is almost eight o'clock."

She looked at the wall clock above their double basin kitchen sink and saw that indeed it was almost time. Klem handed her the mug of freshly brewed coffee and asked, "Will the good lad be coming in? You know he is always welcome, just as if he is a member of our family."

"Thank you for saying that, Dad. No, we will be talking on the front porch for a while. Then he will be off to work. I think he is building a shed for the Thompsons somewhere across town."

Klem wondered what his daughter and Lloyd would be talking about but did not ask. She gently rubbed her dad's arm a few times, then walked toward the door. Abby blew on the top of her coffee to cool it a little then took a sip. She was careful to open the front door and screen so it didn't make a noise. Once outside, she didn't sit but focused her eyes down the street where Lloyd would be coming in his truck. Within a few minutes, his familiar dark-blue truck came into view; then, it turned into the driveway. Abby went down the steps and met him with a kiss and hug. Silently, they both walked up to the porch and sat down. Lloyd nervously looked around while exhaling a large breath.

"Now, Lloyd, darling. I see that you are a little worried about this morning. Please let me honestly reassure you that I love you so very much. I have love for you more than any woman could have for a man."

Lloyd took in another large breath, then slowly let it out. Once again feeling a little more relaxed. Abby squeezed Lloyd's shoulder a couple times and said, "Remember back a few weeks when we went up our lighthouse and stood outside on the railing? I said that I had a decision that might change my life. I also said that you would be the first one to know. This is why I asked you to be with me this morning.

"See, four years ago, I had made a long-standing pack with my college roommate. We promised to each other that we would leave our hometowns and make it big in New York City. We were both freshman English majors with an emphasis in journalism and creative writing. As you know, it has been a few months since we both graduated. By the way, her name is Terri.

"So, after graduation, Terri went home for only a few weeks. Then, she set off to find her fame in the Big Apple. So far, she has done really well. Just in that short time since college, Terri landed her dream job in Manhattan for a magazine called *New York Trend.* But the first thing she did was to find an apartment in the lower east side of Manhattan.

"She said that at least for a while, she will have to live with a girl roommate or maybe even two others. You know what she means, to split the cost of renting and such. Terri feels very lucky to find an apartment with a female who also was looking for a second or even a third roommate.

"So…back to her job. As soon as she got her foot in the door and gained some respect as a journalist, she approached her boss about hiring me. As she explained it in her letter, her boss is very, very busy. To even talk to him about me even once was lucky. As it turns out, she bumped into him at a café downtown during lunch. She talked his ear off about me. In her letter, Terri went on to write that maybe just to salvage his lunchtime, he agreed to give me a chance on a trial basis.

"Well, not to understate it, but I know Terri is so overjoyed and excited. I am sure she could have danced the polka for the rest that week. She believes everything we talked about in college and what we promised to each other is finally coming true.

"Besides landing this fantastic job for which she studied four years in college, Terri and I will be working in the same place and living together. Terri approached her roommate as soon as she got a commitment from her boss about me, even though it was just with a trial basis. Terri tells me that her roommate's name is Nancy, and she also writes for the *New York Trend*. Besides the three of us working for the same magazine, they were also thrilled to finally have a total of three roommates. This was something that they have been looking for, but with no success until now.

"Lloyd, please face me and look into my eyes. I hope you can understand how I can't just ignore this offer from my old roommate. Terri and I shared so many dreams, ambitions, and goals for those four years. Sharing them with each other helped us work even harder on our studies. During the weekends, even when other girls in our dorms were chasing boys and going out drinking and partying, we 'partied' by having a quiet glass of wine. There we were, sharing a little wine in our suite's common area next to the empty washing machines. After the wine, I think we went to bed earlier than everyone. Not later.

"See, my man-friend, Terri and I were good for each other. We truly excelled with our hard-earned studies. We were not in competition with each other. We supported each other all the way. Many times, I can recall that we asked each other to check our writing assignments for misspellings, grammar, and content."

Lloyd felt that he could now ask questions that were burning inside of his heart.

"Please understand, Abby. I am not trying to convince you not to go...not really. But what is your plan? Are you going to New York City and leave me? And if you do, would it be forever? Would I never see you again? How about Parker? What will happen to that little guy?"

"Lloyd, slow down. I don't know the answers to your questions. It hurts me to say that because you deserve to know the answers to all your concerns. I wish I could sit here and answer them all truthfully at this very time. Honey, this is the plain truth. I just do not know. I am in a real dilemma here, and I just ask for your patience.

"If you were telling me the same thing I have just said to you, well, I know I could trust you. Can I have your word that you will trust me? Even more importantly, can you trust our relationship and our love for each other?"

Goodbye

Almost like an impending doom, it was Friday, and time to take Abby to the train station for her future in New York City. Because Lloyd's truck was packed with wood and tools, even in the passenger's seat, Klem and Jane offered their SUV for transportation. In some way, they both thought it would be easier for them and Parker to say goodbye at their house.

They all met on that same front porch of the Watercrests. It seemed that so much of life had occurred on that well-worn structure. In the past one hundred years, it was a place for soothing one's soul, and for many, a needed rest. Other times, it was a sanctuary for thinking and planning. It "saw" much affection between friends and neighbors, but now, it served as a place to say goodbye.

Abby knew this was a three- or four-day fact-finding trip for her, but it could quite possibly lead to forever. Whether or not it was the best thing to do, she wanted to make this goodbye, as some people say, "short and sweet."

While Klem, Jane, and Parker stood on the porch in a line, hugs were shared, except for Parker. He started to cry like a newborn baby. Abby picked him up and held him in her arms.

"Now, Parker, honey. I will only be gone for a few days, four at the most. By next Sunday, I will be back. Now look at me, little son of mine. Be sure that you will be good, and mind your grandparents while I am gone. Make me proud. Okay?"

With having an assignment to *be good*, he composed himself, and Abby gently put him down. Looking for a little more comfort, Parker reached for his grandmother's hand. He looked up at Jane then Klem as if they had an answer for him as to why his mom was going away.

So, backing down the driveway, then onto the street, that scene was the last image she had to take with her to the city. Silence traveled with them all the way to train station. Ten minutes later after they arrived, Lloyd parked Klem's SUV and got out to open the door for Abby. They did not talk until they saw way in the distance, the diesel engine pulling the silver-sided passenger-train cars. Lloyd felt a little numbness inside but then tried to show some understanding spirit.

"Hey there, lovely lady, I hope you enjoy seeing your college friend again. I am sure she has a lot of things to share with you. They say New York City is really something else."

By that time, the train cars had arrived at the station and had completely stopped. The conductor from the passenger car placed a yellow block on the train depot platform for the passengers. One by one, each person stepped up on the block then onto the train. When the last one was on the train, except for Abby, she looked at Lloyd and said, "Hey, big guy, don't hit your thumb with your hammer while I am gone. At least wait when I come back so I can kiss it and make it all better. Remember, I love you to the moon and back."

She gave him a hug and a kiss that he would never forget, then turned around and entered the passenger car just as the conductor called out "Last call, all aboard."

Abby boarded the train car and walked through the center aisle until she found a full empty seat where Lloyd could see her from the train platform outside. She quickly placed her luggage on the seat nearest the aisle and sat next to the window. Because of the light mist that started to coat the window, she never saw him waving goodbye.

Within a short while, the conductor started his walk through the entire train, asking for tickets. Abby retrieved hers from her red leather purse and gave it to him. Thanking her, he punched it with a paper punch and placed it into a holder on her seat. Other than this, there was nothing else going on around her.

Since it was still early in the morning, most of the other passengers were in different stages of sleeping. Because she did not bring a book to read, she tried to get some sleep for herself. Never thinking that sleep would happen, Abby gave out a little sigh and decided to recline and try an attempt. The rocking back and forth of the train on its tracks finally won out and made her fall asleep.

Many hours later, Abby awoke with a start and a little jump when the train made a short stop. Of course, she did not know it, but they were trading the diesel engine for an electric engine to pull the cars through the underground tunnel. For the next ten miles, there was nothing to see out the window, and those that had made the trip before started to gather their things.

The conductor came back into the car she was in. As he walked past Abby and down the aisle, he announced in a loud voice, "Fifteen minutes to our last stop, New York City at Grand Central Station. Please check for all your luggage and belongings. All passengers will be leaving from the rear door of the car."

CHAPTER
17

Dealing with It

Over the next week, Lloyd knew what he had to do for himself. To help make the time seem to go faster, he just had to keep busy. The physical exertion from sawing, hammering, and drilling for his construction project would also help him a lot. He started right at eight in the morning, and except for water breaks and lunch, he literally did not stop for more than ten minutes.

A few weeks ago, Lloyd had lined up a job for Dr. Deloris Lowell and her husband, Sam. After reviewing the plans and cost with them, they sealed the agreement with a simple handshake. Lloyd believed that this was all that was necessary, no written contracts were needed for him.

Since Lloyd always had his truck packed and ready to go with tools, lumber, and hardware, he headed to the doctor's home early that morning. After arriving and pulling out his tools from the passenger's seat, he went to work on their backyard deck. The day melted away while the project took form. He was still going at a grand pace, even into dinnertime. In fact, Lloyd was even thinking of setting up some utility work lights to keep going past dusk.

Sam came home from work at 7:00 p.m. and went out back to see the construction progress. He couldn't believe his eyes. Lloyd was way ahead of his promised deadline but was still cutting wood nearly in the dark. Sam scratched his head and said, "Good heavens, and a bucket of seaweed to boot, Lloyd! Not that I am unhappy that my raised wood patio will be done a week or more early, but you need to get home and rest a little, young man!"

Lloyd finished his cut with his skill saw and looked up at Sam. He couldn't remember the last time he was called *young man.*

"Maybe you are right, I probably should call it a day."

Sam looked around at his partly finished deck. It surely looked awesome. Besides the quality of Lloyd's work, he liked how Lloyd matched the architectural style with the rest of his home.

While they made small talk, Dr. Lowell joined them onto the deck. With admiration in her eyes, she said, "Out on this beautiful deck, I can just imagine entertaining our friends here and even my associate doctors from the practice. It is a perfect place, especially since our backyard has so many overhanging trees. It is almost as if we will have a roof over our heads."

She strolled around the perimeter of the deck, admiring his work, then walked back.

"Now, Lloyd, would you like to stop for the day to have some of my world-famous meat loaf with Sam and me? I always make a two-pounder so we certainly have enough for even three or four more guests."

Lloyd stood up from his kneeling position and shook off the sawdust from his clothing. He wiped his forehead with a hanky that he took from his back pocket.

"You know Dr. Lowell…that is mighty fine of you. If you are sure that is not too much trouble, I would really appreciate your offer a lot."

"I'm extending this invitation to you as long as you call me *Deloris.* Whenever I hear someone address me as *doctor,* I feel like I am still at work. So come on in the house, Lloyd. If you would like to freshen up, I will show you where our guest bath is located."

So people were always kind to Lloyd both for the good work he did for them but also his gentleness and kindness.

Sitting around the dinner table as the food was being passed around and plates were filled, the three of them talked about pleasantries. Sam looked at his wife and said, "Honey, you really look tired today. Did you have a hard day at the clinic?"

"Sam, you are such a dear, thanks for asking. Yes, it's not seeing patients that make things so frustrating. As we have talked before, having seven complete clinics in this part of the state makes it nearly impossible to sustain worthwhile communication between each one. It is frustrating, and in fact, almost impossible. We really need to have a managerial meeting to decide something. Zoom calls just don't cut it. Sometimes patients would be better served at one of our other clinics instead of the one they were going to. Sometimes it seems that one hand doesn't know what the other hand is doing.

"I should stop talking about my work. I don't think Lloyd wants to hear about my frustrations. Now, Lloyd. You are such a dear, working as hard as a bumble bee out there. And like I said, it truly looks absolutely fabulous. I love the handmade railing that you started on the far end. You must be very proud of the way you apply your skill and talent."

"Thank you, Deloris, I approach all my work as if I was doing it for some great competition. To coin a phrase, *it drives me off my pier* if something is not as perfect as I could do it. So if that happens when I am putting it together, and it sometimes does, I back out the wood screws, take it apart, and do it again."

Sam thought that Lloyd's woodworking philosophy was *right on*, so he told him so. Then, after tasting another bit of meatloaf, he asked, "How's that lovely woman friend of yours? That is one fine lady. Not a lot of them like her in the sea, so to say."

"Yes, she is a real darling, and I also love Parker, that little son of hers. From time to time, we do some things together. Of course, he also has his grandparents, Klem and Jane, whom he loves."

Deloris took one of her homemade dinner rolls from the serving plate and passed it over to Lloyd. She then said, "So, if I remember right, she has recently graduated from college. What is she up to these days? Is she looking for a job any time soon?"

It took Lloyd a while to form the words for an answer, then he just came out with it.

"Abby might be looking for a job, in of all places…New York City."

Both Sam and Deloris did not know how to answer. And for quite a while, there was silence at their table. Sam looked at Deloris then at Lloyd. Trying to make the tone around the dining room a little lighter, he said, "I heard that they sell nice hot salted pretzels right on the streets from little vending carts that they wheel around."

CHAPTER
18

A Taste of the Big Apple

The train slowly made its way to Grand Central Station. It found its place along with six other passenger trains that had arrived from all places around the country.

Abby gathered her luggage and stood in the center aisle with the others. It wasn't very long at all before the line of passengers started to move to the far end of the train car. When it was her turn to exit, the conductor who was already on the outside platform, reached up to her, offering his hand for guidance onto the platform.

She took his hand, then stood there a moment, looking around what seemed to be a maze. It didn't take long for her to decide where she should walk to find the waiting area of the Grand Central Station. She instinctively became part of the sea of humanity and traveled with the crowd to her left. Abby could see the bank of eight brass and glass doors where everyone slowed a little to wait their turn. Once through this passageway, she entered the grand waiting room. Within seconds, the passengers dispersed in all directions as they went their separate ways.

Abby could not help herself and had to stop right where she was to look around and especially to look up. It seemed that the arched ceiling of the station ended a mile over her head. Streams of light made cloudy beams cascading through the windows to the inside.

Besides this visual, Abby became aware of two sounds. The first was the constant clicking of shoes on the floor from hundreds of people walking. The other sound was the echoing male voice announcing over the speaker system. The faceless announcer coming from an unknown location listed the name of the various trains with their respective destinations and gate numbers.

In kind of a circle, Abby turned around to look for the information desk, which Terri said would be in the middle of the huge atrium. That location was where she said they would meet. Abby spied the information desk where a collection of people had gathered for directions. As she walked toward it, Abby saw out of the corner of her eye four men sitting on raised chairs while shoe shiners worked their profession with a flare. She wondered how they could possibly support themselves with what she felt was a lowly job. The faint smell of shoe polish traveled with her for a few seconds.

Terri was to meet her at a quarter after twelve, so Abby stood and waited. She pulled up on her sleeve a little to check her watch.

Suddenly, an excited voice came from her right side. Terri ran up to her with open arms. She was wearing comfortable shoes and carrying her black high heels in her one hand.

"Abby! Abby! Abby! Hello there, my dear! It is so good to see you! How was your train trip? Welcome to the Big Apple!"

Abby nearly tripped over her luggage to receive a huge hug from her friend. She noticed Terri had perfume on, a nice sensation. The clothes she was wearing seemed to be so sophisticated, unlike anything that college girls wear.

"My, look at you, Terri! Your coat is simply beautiful, and that sparkling black scarf is a one of a kind. You look like a million bucks! Just marvelous, my friend."

Terri twirled around like a fashion model once or twice for Abby. "Oh you like it? The coat is a Burberry trench that I picked up few days ago at Saks Fifth Avenue. My scarf is from the Franco Ferrari collection. My shoes? Ha! Sketchers from Port James that I brought to exclusively wear on the bus to work."

Terri held up her black pair of Pradas and added, "My boss wants us to only wear heels at work. He says that it is the professional look that we need to give the office. I'll tell you more about him later on."

"Say, Abby, what would like to do first? I have the next two days off from work to show you the sights, you know, the tourist attractions."

She took a small silk bag out of her coat pocket and carefully slipped her high heels into it. Looking at her Gucci watch, she cheerfully said, "Hey, girlfriend, are you hungry? I'm sure you did not eat any of that awful train food! Goodness, I surely would not. You never know how old or how long that food has been hanging around."

CHAPTER
19

Three Roommates

After visiting several famous places during their wonderful tour of the city, Terri used the surface transportation to get them back to her home in Greenwich Village. Abby was both amazed and full of admiration that her transformed, *cosmopolitan* girlfriend could get around one of America's biggest cities with ease.

As the two stepped off the bus and onto the sidewalk, the three-story brown brick apartment building stood before them. Terri lightly took Abby's hand and turned toward her to say, "Well, here we are, what do you think? Isn't it wonderful? I feel very fortunate that my boss lined me up with my roommate and this great place. Of course, everyone has their faults, but Mr. Gram, as he likes to be called, was indispensable to getting me settled. It is only $1,600 a month. If you decide to live here with us, dividing that up three ways, would be very affordable.

"At first, I was looking in Manhattan, but the average seven hundred-square-foot apartment is $3,500 a month for rent. Besides being less expensive to live in the village, as we call it, we are only a short bus ride to work. My office building is just west of Central Park, right near Fordham University and Lincoln Center."

Abby couldn't help but think about how a person in Port James could rent a whole Victorian home for four or maybe five hundred dollars.

Using her apartment front door key card, they entered the small lobby. Terri stopped by a wall of thirty brass boxes each having a small window with a number stenciled on it. She moved her finger from left to right on the third row until she came to her mailbox. She was able to stand on tiptoes to see if there was anything in hers. Seeing nothing, she said, "Maybe my roommate already took in the mail."

They walked a few more steps to the apartment elevator and touched the "Up" button. As they waited, Terri said, "So, Abby, I am on the third floor. Sometimes I have to take the steps, but I see the elevator is working again."

A bell announced the arrival of the elevator, and the doors opened. Arriving on the third floor, the elevator once again opened. They both walked down a hallway that had well-worn carpeting and was slightly musty smelling. Finding her key in her purse, she inserted it in her door and pushed it open with her foot.

Just as soon as they entered, Nancy came from the kitchen area to greet them.

"Hi, Nancy, here is Abby. As I told you over these past several weeks, she was my best friend from college. And as you also remember, she wants to relocate here and work for the *New York Trend Magazine* in our group. Teddy wants to talk with her on Thursday."

Nancy asked, "Teddy? Did you call Mr. Gram, *our boss*, Teddy? Did he actually allow you to call him that?"

Nancy seemed totally amazed at Terri's reference to their boss. She would not let this issue stop without resolving itself.

"Well, Mr. Gram really liked my last article for the Living Here section. He surprised me in my cubicle and gave me a big bear hug and several kisses on my lips. He also winked at me, then he said, "Good work, girl. If you do more features like that, a raise could be coming your way. But for now, you can call me Teddy.""

Nancy responded, "Several kisses? You naughty girl! But you are one *lucky* naughty girl."

Abby had a complete astonished look on her face, which she hoped that Nancy or Terri did not noticed. In order to change the conversation, she said, "Can I see the rest of your apartment?"

Nancy went back to the kitchen area where she was heating up some canned soup on the stove. She turned around and said to Abby, "Well, my new roommate, this is just about all of it."

In a kidding way, but in truth, she pointed around the room, saying, "As you can see, over there is our window. This wall where I am standing is our kitchen, and that convertible couch next to the entrance is our living room. Down our hallway are two bedrooms and the bathroom we share. That's about it! Oh, there are closets—"

Terri interrupted Nancy, "Hey, girlfriend, you took the wind out of my sails! I wanted to give her the big tour, but I have to admit, you did a good job."

* * * * *

Nancy's soup was passable, but the bread she served was spectacular. Abby did not realize how much of an appetite she had, probably from Terri's walking tour around town. After taking her second slice of bread, she asked, "This bread is marvelous! Where did you find it?"

Nancy said, "Well thank you. Just down the street from us is a little bakery where they make this bread and tons of sweet stuff. See, even though we live in this huge city, there are small communities that are unique. They are like little village neighborhoods among the busyness of the Big Apple. They have their own hardware stores, small grocery stores, specialty shops, doctor's offices, and so on. Most of these businesses are privately owned and are not a chain store. It makes it so interesting to live here. Oh, of course there are many wonderful ethnic restaurants where everyone knows you. Let's see, to name a few neighborhoods besides our own, there is our own Greenwich Village, Little Italy, Chinatown, The Bowery, Soho, East Village, and a few others."

Abby said, "Well that sounds just delightful! I can see why you like city living."

Now it was Terri's turn to add something.

"Nancy, you never asked me why I was so late coming home from work yesterday. Let me tell you and Abby what happened. I had to take the subway home from an assignment in Harlem. For my article, I was interviewing a doctor who works in the Mount Sinai Medical Center. I had the article all done and ready to send from my laptop rather early. It was only seven o'clock."

Abby looked perplexed about her saying *early*. Terri noticed and explained that they usually are expected to be at work at 9:00 a.m. but stay till 9:00 p.m. most weekdays.

"Okay, so I got seated on the subway, and we were headed to the next stop. Just before the train came to the station, the wheels squealed loudly with the brakes on. Our darn subway car went abruptly into a full stop. We stayed there, not moving for almost forty-five whole minutes. As it turns out, a guy committed suicide by throwing himself, head first, right on the tracks just in front of our train. Terrible! But…why did he have to do it during rush hour for heaven's sake? Really? It slowed down several subway lines for quite a while. Rush hour, really?"

Abby still loved Terri but felt that she picked up a little *hard skin* nature. For Abby, hearing her story made her feel so sorry for the unfortunate fellow who killed himself. She also thought about his family who would have been waiting for him to come home. Terri then wanted to lighten the conversation a little and reminisced about their college activity in their junior year.

"Nancy, did you know that Abby, sitting across from you this very moment, and I were in a regatta sailing club at school? It was in our third year at college."

Turning to Abby, she said, "We sure had some fun, didn't we? The two of us thought we were pretty cool."

"Terri, I have never forgotten that. In fact, for my birthday, Lloyd paid for the rental of a single-person Sunfish for three whole hours. You know, it only took a short time to get the knack of it all over again. While I was maneuvering the small waves out there in the water that we call Big Duck Inlet, I thought of us the whole time."

Terri got up from the table and, while staying in place, acted out the motions of working the waves on her single-person sailboat. Both Nancy and Abby laughed at her drama. Once again, Abby had that special excited sparkle in her eyes and added, "Right on, girlfriend! And after we got good at it, how many times did we play Frisbee with each other while we sailed along? Gosh, that was really something, we just loved every minute of it. We must have gone out on the water thirty times that year!"

Terri sat back down at the table while both of them saw scenes of those precious outings play vividly in their minds. Then Nancy spoke up, "Maybe you both do not know this, but the Big Apple has several sailing clubs. When the weather was nice on Saturdays, I use to watch them practice using those small dinghies. The most prominent yacht club is simply called *The New York Yacht Club*. It is far from simple, however. It was founded in 1844. Their club was first located in Hoboken, New Jersey, right on the Hudson River. Later on, the club moved to West 55th Street. The place is more beautiful than most castles in Europe. In fact, the clubhouse is a *national historical landmark*.

"It also has connections with a yacht club in Newport, Rhode Island. The membership is truly for the rich and famous. They hosted the annual regatta race presented by Rolex. The club also sponsored an invitational for amateurs and numerous other team racing events.

"Now I think that if either of you would like to sail again, you should check out some of the lesser expensive clubs. You might not even have to be a member to rent a single-person sailboat. What did you call it? A Sunfish?"

The three friends all had some more bread and entertained some quiet thoughts of their own. Then Nancy broke the silence and made a little chuckle as she introduced a story of her own.

"Now, girls, it goes without saying that we have the best subway system. Taking advantage of the surface transportation, the elevated lines, and the subways, you can manage without a car. So with that said, people, well...women especially, need to have subway smarts.

"Last week, on the subway, I was sitting across from a lady who had placed her purse on the bench seat. It was wedged between her leg and the man's leg who was sitting right next to her. You know how crowded it can be. So…anyways without her knowing, the man next to her had his hand in her purse. He was obviously trying to steal something from it. The lady finally noticed and started yelling at the man, who quietly just sat up, and casually walked away from her, like nothing happened!

"Now, Abby, when we girls ride the subway or bus, we know to place our purse on our lap, with both hands on the top."

Terri agreed, then had another story.

"A few days ago, I was not on the subway but was riding the elevated train across from a lady passenger. I could not believe it, but the man sitting next to her on the bench seat started to place his hand on her leg. Right then and there, that man who was a total stranger to her started caressing this lady's leg. Well, to my surprise, she grabbed his hand and raised it high in the air, saying, 'Whose hand is this?' Well, after pulling his hand out of the air and from her grasp, that worthless creep stayed cool. He pretended to fall asleep! Yes! He faked sleeping with his mouth open and eyes shut! Just like this!"

Terri mimicked the way he looked having her mouth open, eyes shut, and rocking her head to-and-fro, like being on the train. Then she opened her eyes again and said, "The nerve of some people, can you imagine that?"

Abby felt that she was getting a real education while eating here with these girls. Both of them looked at innocent, small-town Abby, with her wide-eyed expression. Nancy reached across the table and held Abby's hands and said, "Now, Abby, this city is a wonderful place to live. There is so much diversification and talented people. Our medical centers are first rate, and entertainment is unmatched anywhere. Don't you agree, Terri?"

Terri nodded yes and said, "Of course."

Nancy then added, "Abby, you just have to be *street smart.* Okay?"

Abby thought that there was so much to learn if she moved here. She was happy that Terri would always be her friend. With a compassionate look for Abby, Terri said, "I just have to tell you, my friends, that for my lunch, I did something a little different. Instead of eating at my cubicle and still working, I took a short walk around Lincoln Center for the Performing Arts. You know that is about three streets west of Central Park. They must have been doing a little advertising for tonight's symphony performance. Some of the musicians got together, and right on the outside courtyard, they were playing the most beautiful classical pieces. I believe it was Bach or Beethoven. I was fortunate to find an empty park bench, and I took it all in. It truly was one of the most inspirational and uplifting lunches that I had ever experienced."

Abby thought that for the first time of this visit, this was a little glimmer of her friend's tender side. Just then, Abby's cellphone rang. It was where she had placed it on the couch upon her arrival. Having Lloyd's ring tone, Abby's heartbeat quickened as she had a vision of Lloyd's handsome face. Terri and Nancy watched as she skipped over to her phone to swiftly answer it.

"Oh, honey! How are you doing? Yes, I miss you too. Really? You are finishing up on that project already? What? You want to come down and be with me for Thursday and Friday?"

By this time, Nancy and Terri started to clean up the table and put the dishes on the kitchen counter. They wanted to give Abby as much privacy that they could in their small studio apartment. Terri started the water for the sink, and Nancy took a cloth towel from under the sink to start drying.

After about twenty minutes, Abby made kissing sounds into her phone and hung up. She had that sparkle in her eyes and that rosy flush to her complexion that showed she was in love. Terri gave her a minute to sit at the kitchen table, then asked, "So how is your man doing, you lucky girl?"

"Oh, he truly is heavenly, I love him so. That man of mine just gave me a surprise! He wants to come here on Thursday and Friday! I told him that I will try to find a hotel room to stay that hopefully would not be too far from here."

Talking at the same time in different ways, Nancy and Terri announced to her that he would never, under any circumstances, have to sleep in a hotel."

Terri explained, "That couch makes up into a bed. We use it occasionally for guests. When my mom came to visit, it worked out just fine. She said it was surprisingly comfortable. As you saw from your extensive apartment tour, Nancy and I sleep in the same bedroom. The other bedroom is for our clothes. However, we can make room in that second bedroom for you to sleep. Now this is the end of our discussion. It is all set! We can't wait to meet that hunk!"

CHAPTER
20

Some Planning

Nancy was second to get up, showered, and dressed, all ready to go to work. They allowed Abby to sleep in, while Terri was already at the kitchen table writing an article for the magazine. Nancy looked at her business appearance once more in the wall mirror. She adjusted her scarf around her neck, then had a frown on her face. Turning around, Nancy asked Terri, "Does this scarf go with my blouse? I think it does, but I need your opinion."

Terri looked up from her laptop and analyzed her attire. "I think it is fine, but you have a little smudge on the top of your left high heels. Aside from that, I think Mr. Gram will like it."

With one shoe off and one on, Nancy hobbled over to the kitchen sink to wash the mark off her shoe. Then after adjusting her dress belt, she went to the door. Turning to Terri, she jokingly said, "So when I get to the office, I will give *Teddy* your love."

Terri rolled her eyes and said while delivering a smile, "I will see you at work in a few hours, but now, get the heck out of here, you beautiful female!"

Nancy gave Terri a little naughty wiggle, and a delightful laugh, as she went out the door and into the hallway.

By this time, Abby came from the guest room and into the kitchen. Looking around, she said, "Good morning! I am sorry I slept in. I must have missed Nancy. I was really more tired than I thought I was."

Earlier, Terri made some coffee and had placed some breakfast rolls on the table for all of them. Now that her college girlfriend was sitting next to her, she closed her laptop and moved it aside to eat with her.

"Now isn't this nice, Abby! Us two having breakfast, just like at school!"

Abby recalled their long conversations about their goals, aspirations, and dreams when they were in their dorm room and had finished studying.

"Say, Terri, I sure have missed you since college. And I can't thank you enough for all you have done for me...for us."

"Hey, what are pinky finger friends for? As I wrote to you, I have put in a good word for you with Mr. Gram. Now he truly is busy, but he wants to see you for an opening he has in our section. Later on this afternoon, he will be available to talk with you. I am guessing that should be around five o'clock."

"Terri, you are a magical woman. Again, thank you! Can I lay this other thing on you?"

Terri said, "Certainly."

"Well, I believe that Lloyd is another answer to my dreams. He seems to have been brought into my life directly from God. I truly love him. So, besides landing a lifelong dream job here in New York City at *The New York Trend*, I could not imagine my life without him. But, Terri, my friend, how could this ever work with us? Is there any work here in the city that needs his skills?"

"Now, girlfriend, I knew you would never leave him, even for a dream job in your journalistic writing field. So I asked my coworkers around the office and eventually talked with Jill. She is a lovely, middle-aged woman who is the receptionist for our office suite. Her husband is also a woodworker.

"They made it happen by living near the Brooklyn Campus of Polytech University. He does construction both in Queens and Brooklyn. Of course, that means that Jill has to commute every day, but she has gotten used to it. Besides, her hubby loves living in

Brooklyn, and the jobs are endless. Jill says that whenever he puts his woodworking advertisement in the local paper, he gets so many calls that he is booked up for several months."

Abby had a tear in her eye from the appreciation she had for Terri.

"Besides all that, the other day, she said that he might be looking for either a helper or a partner, not sure, really. I think he is a little older than Jill, maybe sixty years old, and would like to take it a little easier. With a partner, or whatever, it could work for him very nicely.

"How about this? When I get to the office, I will talk with Jill some more about your Lloyd. I could probably do that during her break time.

"Now girlfriend, I need to get my little derriere on the bus and get to work. I have a list of places you can visit around town. Just have fun, and I will see you *when the cows come home*. For heaven's sake, where did I dig up *that* expression? I think it was from my grandfather. Ha!"

CHAPTER
21

Looking Around and More

It was a pleasant day to be in the Big Apple. It was not hot at all. A nice cool breeze bathed the streets and avenues. Abby walked around Greenwich Village, almost afraid to venture any farther. She noticed with interest that there were a number of small playhouses that were presenting stage performances. They all hoped that theirs would become a success. They were known as *Off-Broadway plays*, where some influential performing agents attend to look for local talent.

Outside one of the playhouses, a street performer dressed in a black tuxedo was juggling five bowling pins. Another group of people were singing some Broadway songs from the musical *Cats*. They had painted on kitty whiskers and pinned-on furry tails on their backside. It seemed to Abby that everyone had a story to tell.

Since the streets were so entertaining, Abby could not believe that when she looked at her watch, it was well into lunchtime. Just near Washington Square was a little restaurant that had outside seating with roundtables and tall chairs. Surprisingly, Abby noticed that there was no available seating either inside or outside. Nevertheless, she took a menu from a stack that was lying on a pedestal near the entrance. While glancing at each page, a young male waiter instantly came out and welcomed Abby. He offered the three-page menu even though she already had one in her hand. He seemed pleasant but somehow in a hurry. Without asking, he said something to a lady customer who had just been taken to one of the outside roundtables. She seemed to agree with the waiter, and then with a little flair, he directed Abby to the lady's table.

When Abby sat down, she looked a little more at the menu, then at the lady who was only three feet across from her. After a short silent time, Abby said, "I am so sorry to barge in on you. I feel a little odd to take half of this table of yours. I mean, you were here first."

Looking above her rhinestone reading glasses, the lady looked at Abby and said, "You are not from around here, are you? I thought so, honey. This happens all the time in New York. If everyone waited for their own table, there would not be enough time to eat. It is just the way it is in a big city, not just New York City, really *any* large one."

Abby felt a little more at ease and said, "Oh I see. I didn't know. And yes, I am not from around here, I am from Port James, Maine."

"Hmm…a bit of a distance to have lunch. Don't they have restaurants in Maine?" The lady introduced herself as Florence and then just continued to talk as if they were best of friends.

"I remember when I was relocating to this city from Oswego. Oswego is up on Lake Ontario, you know. Well, I still had a car, a 1999 Ford of some kind. See, I later found that I didn't need a car in the city, too expensive to park. Do you know that renting a parking spot in a garage can run you up to one thousand dollars every month? The New York City Parking Authority says that the monthly average cost of one silly outside parking space is over four hundred dollars. Can you imagine that?"

At this point, the waiter came back and took their order, then spun around on his heels and into the restaurant to the kitchen.

"So let me tell you how naïve I was. I picked up one of those home listing magazines you see in some store entrances. You know, they feature properties for sale. Well, flipping through it, I found a bargain. The small place was out at the tip of Long Island, near Montauk Point. It was a little fishing cabin, about six hundred square feet, not much bigger than this patio where we are sitting."

Florence combed her fingers through her hair a few times, then continued her account.

"I think you needed to bring in bottled water, but at least, there was electrical service to the place. It was listed for *only twenty thousand dollars.* I say, twenty thousand, yes, that is a real bargain! I figured that I would settle out there, fix it up, and forget this city. When I called about the particulars, I was told that twenty grand was only to rent the darn thing for one summer. Can you believe that? All that hard-earned money for only three summer months! Good Lord, I said to myself, this is one expensive place to live! Good thing I met a downtown lawyer and married him so we could afford a place around here in the village, as we call it. His office practice is in Manhattan specializing in accident lawsuits."

The waiter came back with their lunches and drinks. As he placed the dishes down on their small table, he asked, "Is there anything else I can get for you, nice ladies?"

He paused at their table; then, Florence dismissed him with a flick of her hand and continued, "Handsome waiter, don't you think? Nice too. Probably nice to us so that we give him a large tip. So what was I going to say? Oh yes. Last week, I read about something that happened in the Bronx. See, this man's car was about to catch on fire, so he ran across the street to a gas station. He asked for their fire extinguisher so he could cool his overheated engine. Do you know what the gas station owner said? He wouldn't let him have the darn fire extinguisher unless he gave him a thirty-dollar deposit. The desperate man quickly reached into his wallet and gave him a credit card, but the guy said they only took cash. Well, the short of it was that he completely lost his car to the flames.

"Just like the poor saps that get a flat tire down on the Cross Bronx Expressway. They are busy changing their tire only to find out that another stranger is stealing the grill from the front of their car. Can you imagine that, even in full daylight? I don't know what is wrong with some people."

Florence took a fork full of her Mediterranean salad and seemed to have one more thought.

"Now, please don't get the impression that all New Yorkers are like that. I can still remember when I first came to the city, I had the most challenging time figuring out the subway system. It seems that when people you meet on the street know something…well, they are so pleased to help you. Most of the time, I was heading to the correct subway entrance, but I was not 100 percent sure. On numerous occasions, when I asked someone on the street, they were so, very nice and helpful."

By this time, Abby had finished her sliced turkey sandwich, so she scooted a ten and a five under her plate. She pulled her chair away from the table, and as she left, she politely thanked Florence for her company.

CHAPTER 22

The Boss

Abby was almost dizzy from the endless stories that Florence shared with her over lunch. It was almost four o'clock, and she had to set out to where Nancy and Terri worked. Even though it would be expensive, she hailed a yellow cab and closed her eyes during the short trip.

In the back seat of the cab, she tried to clear her mind of everything. She needed this short time to feel a little more uplifted and calm. So, as the streets and avenues passed by with sidewalks of clustered people walking at a jogging pace, she said a prayer.

"Dear heavenly Father, thank You for my life and my family… and my Lloyd. I certainly do not know where my life will take me, but I ask You for Your guidance and direction. There are so many aspects of this city…both good and…bad. I really need Your help. So please be with me today and always. Amen."

The taxi arrived at 73rd Street and Columbus Avenue just at the same time Terri came out of her sixty-story office building. Abby gave the driver a twenty, about four dollars more than what the cabbie's meter was showing. As she opened the door and stood on the sidewalk, Terri said, "Well look at you, *city girl*. Taking a taxi all by yourself! No ride sharing for you! Pretty uptown classy!"

Abby didn't feel classy, but together with the prayer she sent to God from the taxi's back seat and her girlfriend's compliment, she felt very much uplifted. Terri walked the few steps with her to the building entrance where she pushed through the glass and brass revolving door into the central lobby.

"Here we are, Abby, one elevator ride to my *home away from home*. This is a fast elevator, not like at my apartment, so hold on to your stomach."

The elevator went straight up to the twenty-fifth floor without stopping on any of the others. When the elevator doors opened, Abby saw the reception desk with a little note indicating that she would be right back. Behind her desk, Abby saw a sea of green cubicles that seemed to go on forever. Terri motioned for Abby to follow her. They walked past some washrooms, a conference room, and the floor's break room. Some of the more fortunate people working in the cubicles near the windows had a beautiful view of Central Park and the city's skyline beyond the park. The buildings seemed to glow in the distance.

Terri stopped at the first of only three offices, which was Mr. Gram's. She knocked on his window lightly to get his attention. Saying goodbye to his wife on the phone, he motioned for Terri to come in. Abby stayed outside the closed door of the boss's office. After they talked a few minutes, Abby saw Terri turn around and wave to her to come in. Abby took a deep breath and pulled opened the door to enter.

Mr. Gram, an overweight man with a bad comb-over to hide his bald spot, extended his hand for his greeting. Abby thought that he held her hand a little too long, and she instantly wanted to pull it away. She felt the moisture that came from his fleshy hand and was now on hers. Abby wanted to wipe it away but did not want to offend him.

"So, Abby, my girl here has told me a lot of wonderful things about you. I guess you both were college dorm roommates. Are all the girls at your college as pretty as you? If I was only five years younger and attending college…"

Abby thought, *Five years?* She surmised that the guy had to be fifty years old.

"So, this is what I am planning for you, Abby. Since I am taking Terri's recommendation about you, I will forgo a formal interview. In the next week or so, send me an original article of your own. It should be suitable for the travel section of our magazine. If I like it, we can talk further about employment. If not, you can find work at one of our competitors, not that there are any."

"Hey, that's a joke! No other magazine comes close to our standard. Seriously, I have a lot of *great girls* working here for me."

Mr. Gram then gave her a smothering hug and said, "Now remember that article you need to send me. It will either make you or break you."

The girlfriends left his office and headed back to the elevators. Abby thought to herself that the few minute encounter with Terri and Nancy's boss must have lasted for more than an hour.

CHAPTER
23

The Assignment

Abby decided to go directly back to the apartment to write the article for Mr. Gram. She knew that both Nancy and Terri would be at work, so the apartment would be quiet. However, on the way back, she got off the bus a few blocks early to enjoy some of the ambiance of Greenwich Village. Terri and Nancy were correct. The cluster of shops made a close neighborhood feeling. People could find anything they needed including small but well-stocked grocery stores. She liked the slower pace as compared to Manhattan. While passing most people on the sidewalk, they actually exchanged smiles with her.

While doing this little walking tour, Abby strolled by a small grade or middle school. The small-aged children were kicking a ball around in their school courtyard while close by, several teachers were monitoring their play. It was pleasurable to hear the laughter of the little children at play. The entire activity appeared to be well controlled, and the scene reassured Abby if Parker was enrolled there.

Stepping out of her comfort zone, Abby waved to one of the teachers. They looked at each other, and then one walked up to Abby. She gave a smile and said, "Hello, can I help you with anything?"

Abby saw that the teacher had a small notebook in her left hand, and with her right arm, she extended a handshake.

"My name is Abby, and I am considering a move to this area. I have a six-year-old son and have some concern about his schooling. It seems that the children I see here appear very happy."

"Nice to meet you, Abby. My name is Karen. Yes, our students truly like being here. Our teachers have created educational programs that encourage developmental success in a healthy and safe environment. We have enrichment programs offering physical activity, arts, and crafts, and of course, cognitive development. If your child is enrolled here, I am sure he would enjoy our school. If you would like to schedule a tour, I can give your name and telephone number to our school principal."

Abby thanked her and said that when the times comes, she certainly will love a tour. Karen looked over toward the children and excused herself.

"Nice meeting you, Abby. Our classroom period will be starting soon, maybe we will meet again."

This whole encounter gave Abby a little skip in her step. Soon she was back at the apartment entrance. It almost felt like home when she opened the outside door and went inside to take the stairs. When she opened the apartment door, Abby strolled over to the living room window. She looked at the activity on the street. It was full of automobiles, and the sidewalks were crowded with pedestrians walking by. Just minutes ago, she was down there and part of it all. Gazing some more, she assumed that most of them lived here, and from her vantage point, they seemed relatively happy. Still looking out of the window, she thought to herself, *I could describe my dilemma as a huge if in my life. If I move here, I think I can handle the forward advances of Mr. Gram. The work at the magazine is right up my alley. My precious son, whom I love so much, will eventually adjust. I think.*

She turned around and went over to the kitchen table and sat down with her computer opened and ready. As she gazed at the home screen, her thoughts continued.

I would never come here to make my mark unless Lloyd was here too. The thought of eventually living in Brooklyn seemed appealing even though I would have a long commute. It would be worth it knowing that Lloyd would be able to do his construction work for a living.

The image in her mind of Lloyd cutting wood, driving nails, and even taking a break to give his well-developed muscles a little rest made her heart beat a little faster.

Taking in a large breath, Abby exhaled slowly and fully several times. She learned that relaxing technique from her yoga classes at college.

"Well, I guess this is where I am. If Lloyd stays with me, it is a done deal…I think."

Abby started to regress into more images, this time of Klem and Jane sadly sitting alone at their breakfast table. She envisioned them looking at each other, then silently sharing the view through their kitchen window at the lighthouse.

"Oh God! Can I do that to my parents? Can I do that to me? What about Parker? He would miss them so."

Abby knew she needed to concentrate on the job at hand. The article had to be written and sent electronically to the magazine. She did not have a problem with the topic for the magazine's travel section. The words and phrases would come easily, so she rubbed her temples a few times and opened a blank Word page.

The thoughts flew from her fingers and onto the screen, becoming a beautiful work of art. When she finished, she knew her article was truly wonderful. If it became published for subscribers to read, it certainly would bring lovely images with feelings of a charming escape. It would give a well-needed diversion from their own lives.

As she was ready to hit *send*, Abby looked once more at her article's title, "Portland's Enchanting Observation Tower."

CHAPTER
24

Trauma at the Watercrest's Home

Klem and Jane were making another big farm breakfast in their inviting, warm kitchen. Klem said, "Let's see, scrambled eggs, bacon, whole wheat buttered toast, and of course orange juice, and for those old enough, hot coffee."

Jane smiled and said, "Dear, you sound like the breakfast special in the *Tinker's Family Restaurant*."

"Nothing too good for you and Parker. By the way, did you get him up yet?"

Jane touched the tips of her short white hair a little to make sure every strand was in place. That also gave her a few seconds to decide that she would go back upstairs and wake up Parker. Klem said, "Don't take too long to get that little boy, everything is hot and ready to eat."

Jane walked down their hallway and stopped at Parker's bedroom door. She was going to knock but decided to crack open his door to sneak a look. To her surprise, she saw and heard Parker whimpering in his sleep. She quickly tiptoed over to him to softly rub his shoulders to waken him. Instead of waking, poor Parker started yelling and sobbing.

"I want my mommy! I want my mommy!"

Thrashing around in his bed, Jane saw that a portion of his sheets were wet with his perspiration. Trying to secure his shoulders, she reached for him, pulling her grandson into a hug for comfort and reassurance. Still crying, Parker finally awoke and wrapped his little arms around his grandma.

"Why does my mommy want to move? I love it here, and I would really miss you and grandpa. Are you going to talk with her? Please?"

"Oh, my precious child, Grandpa and I were planning to talk with your mommy when she gets back. Right for now, please remember that our heavenly Father loves us and will always be with us…no matter where we are living on this earth of ours. And also remember, Grandpa and I love you dearly. If you have to move, we will visit as often as we can. Okay, precious?"

From his grandma's reassuring words, Parker felt slightly better. He pulled his sheets and blanket off and placed his feet on the floor. Looking down at them while alternating one on top of the other, he said, "Thank you, Grandma, I love you. Maybe I can eat a little breakfast now. Is Grandpa downstairs?"

"Yes, he is, and I believe he is waiting for us."

CHAPTER
25

A Little Diversion

After breakfast, Parker went outside to fly a little balsawood airplane that Klem had purchased for him on the day his mom left. Last night after dinner, he had helped Parker to put it all together. Klem explained that each piece was very delicate and could easily break. Looking on, he made sure Parker was careful to separate each little section while explaining where each had to go to make the plane. When it was all put together, with beaming pride, Parker sent the little plane flying around the living room.

Klem finished washing the breakfast dishes and was ready to make his walk up to the lighthouse to perform his morning duties. As he was getting his jacket and straw hat from the wooden hook by the back door, Jane asked, "Klem dear, can we talk before you leave to go to work at the lighthouse gift shop? It is about Parker this morning."

Klem put back his hat and sat at the kitchen table. Jane placed herself where she could see Parker playing in the backyard.

"I'm sure you heard some commotion coming from Parker's bedroom. He was in an awful way, having a nightmare."

"Yes, I did hear it and was just about to come up the stairs to see what was wrong, but by that time, both of you were coming down."

Jane placed her hands on both sides of her face. She replayed what had occurred earlier that morning.

"Our poor grandson was crying and totally beside himself because of the possibility of moving to New York City. He was crying for his mommy and thrashing about in his sleep."

"Klem, right then and there, I promised him that we certainly will have a heart-to-heart talk with Abby when she comes back. Gosh, this whole thing is just terrible! Don't you think so, Klem?"

Jane opened her pocket and found a Kleenex to wipe her eyes. She then looked at her loving husband for his agreement about talking to Abby.

Klem reached for Jane, and the two of them hugged in their kitchen. He whispered into her ear and said, "Oh my Good Lord, it sure is terrible."

They both decided to sit at their dining room table to talk a little more. Klem continued, "In a small way, I can understand why our daughter wants to move. After graduating on the dean's list at college and having an opportunity for a journalist job, it must be wonderful. But then, what in the world is she thinking? I just can't believe her leaving a nice, secure place like Port James and all her friends. How about us? Would she just leave us alone to be here without her? And what about Lloyd? What about that relationship? Then what about uprooting our grandson? Could Parker handle it? Wouldn't he miss us nearly every day?"

Klem looked into Jane's worried eyes for a minute, then continued, "Honey, you are right to tell Parker that when she gets back, we will be expressing our feelings about all this with her."

"Thanks, Klem. We certainly will do just that. I almost hate to say this, but of course, our daughter will be making her own decision."

Jane gave Klem a kiss on his cheek, then took both of her hands in his.

"Klem darling, we also need to pray about this too."

Klem got up from the table and, with a heavy heart in his soul, walked to the back door. He breathed out a sigh and retrieved his white straw hat from the wooden hook.

As soon as he opened the door and started up the footpath to his lighthouse, Jane had a thought. She talked a little to herself, then picked up the phone and made a call to Lloyd.

When Lloyd's cell phone rang, he was buying some wood at the lumberyard and was standing in the contractors' checkout line. He answered it as soon as he saw it was from the Watercrest's.

"Hi, Lloyd, are you busy? Got a minute? Great!"

Jane described the morning events that had happened and waited for Lloyd's reaction.

Lloyd swiped his credit card in the cashier's reader and signed his name on the screen. Placing his card back in his pocket, he pulled his wheeled cart out of the lumberyard and into the parking lot. As he started to load his wood onto his truck's bed, he continued his conversation with Jane, "Jane, I have to deliver some lumber for my current woodworking project. After that, I better see Parker. Give me about an hour to get to your home."

Jane hung up and felt a little more lighthearted. She was so pleased that the two of them hit it off so well, enjoying whatever they do. She looked around her home and decided that she would straighten up a little before Lloyd arrived. She walked into the living room and sat on the couch where the coffee table was. She picked up some magazines and catalogues, placing the old ones in one pile to recycle. Then she leaned back on the couch and dozed off.

Lloyd's knock at the door awoke Jane from her unexpected nap. He opened the screen door and asked, "Is there anyone home?"

Jane got up and greeted him; then, they both sat down. Lloyd knew that she had been feeling distraught, and he felt it equally.

"Jane, I have a couple of things to talk to you about. I am taking the rest of today off from my projects and in fact Friday too. As soon as we finish here, I think I would like to take Parker canoeing up along Big Duck Inlet. It is so beautiful, and today the weather is perfect. Parker and I were just there the other day, and he absolutely loved it.

"So that is the first thing. Secondly, I decided to make a trip to be with Abby after her last scheduled day in the city. I called her a couple of days ago, and she was very excited! Since I will be making the trip, your daughter will be coming back a day later than planned. I should have asked you first…but is that okay with you and Klem?

"Of course it is, you don't need our approval. So how are you getting there and back?"

"Well, I am going to fly down, then Abby and I will take the train back home. Do you think that I can get a ride to the Portland airport? Then would you be willing to pick us up at the train station when we arrive back here?"

"That would be fine, we can certainly do that. Um…I thought you were terrified of flying."

"Yes, I am, but I can't wait to see Abby again." He gave Jane a hug and headed back to his truck.

First, he made a short stop at his construction site and unloaded his truck. Then, on his way to the Watercrest's, he stopped at his own house and slid his L.L.Bean Old Town canoe in the back. Pulling out of his drive, he looked at his plastic hula girl on his dash. She seemed to be in agreement that Lloyd should make the trip to be with Abby for two days in the Big Apple. Lloyd said, "Well, little hula, I can see you agree, and thanks for that."

Turning into Klem and Jane's driveway, Parker saw Lloyd's truck with his two-person canoe in the truck bed. He ran up to the front door, pushing it open. Running across the front lawn, he jumped into Lloyd's arms.

"Are we going on a canoe ride? Huh? Are we, Lloyd? Huh?"

26

Canoeing

Lloyd parked his truck at a small grass lot, which had only six parking spaces. Parker and Lloyd got out of the truck and looked at Big Duck Inlet. The water was so calm that it looked like glass. Birds were flying overhead, and some movement could be seen under the inlet water.

"Remember this place, Parker? It was where your mom went sailing. You and I were also here when we sat on the deck that I was making for the gazebo."

"I sure do, it is now one of my favorite places." Parker looked up at the canoe in the bed of the truck and said, "How are we going to get your canoe off the truck?"

Parker was more than eager and ready to follow Lloyd's directions.

"Good question, Parker. Okay. First, I will lower the tailgate like this. Stand back, Parker, while I unlatch the handle and lower the tailgate. Now go around to the other side of the canoe, and I will stay on this side. Ready? Now, we pull."

To Parker's surprise, it came sliding out and onto the grass with ease.

"Now, Parker, with the rope in the front, we can drag the canoe on the grass and onto the pier ahead. Let's go."

There was a single pier for small pleasure craft, and to the right and parallel to it was the commercial pier. Both piers were short since there was no need for them to be any longer. Once they had the canoe on the wooden dock, Lloyd gave Parker an orange child-size life jacket. He helped him snap it on. Satisfied that his little friend's jacket was secure, he then placed his arms through his own and snapped it.

"Okay, Parker, next is the only tricky part of canoeing. I will guide my canoe from the side of this pier and then gently into the water. At this point, I will not let go of it, so when you are ready, go on all fours and carefully crawl onto the canoe. As soon as you are in, sit on the front seat. Now, don't be nervous, but until both of us are seated, the canoe is a little tippy. Okay, go ahead now, Parker, I won't let go of the canoe."

Parker did as Lloyd said and easily found his seat; then, Lloyd reproduced the same maneuver for himself. Using their wooden paddles, they pushed from the dock and slowly went forward.

"Parker, my canoeing friend, you did just fine. Now paddle on one side about ten times, then swing your paddle to the other, again for about ten times. I will steer from the back while also paddling. If we have to turn sharply for some reason, I will back paddle."

After this short class in canoeing, Parker started looking around. The inlet was the home of many fish, animals, and birds. Some were native to Maine; others flew in from places in Canada to stay for a short time. In order to take in the beauty and enjoy nature, Lloyd told Parker to rest his paddle across both gunnels and rest a while. Lloyd did the same.

"See, Parker, just about three o'clock and in the distance are some green winged teal ducks. Aren't they cute? Oh, I should explain, three o'clock is to your right, six would be behind you, nine is to your left, and twelve o'clock is straight ahead, just like the numbers on a clock if you laid it down on your lap."

"Oh, I get it, just like a clock! Hey look! At nine o'clock, what is that beautiful all white bird? Look at its long neck!"

"That is a white crane. Yes, they are pretty and are experts at catching fish. If we are lucky, maybe we can see an Atlantic puffin flying around those cliffs. So we can get a better view, let's paddle out to that area."

Now that they had a mission, the two friends paddled along, cutting through the water quietly but now at a nice speed. In a short time, they were just at the mouth of the inlet and alongside the sandy cliffs of the ocean. Guiding the canoe parallel to the cliffs, they took a rest and waited.

Their silence was broken by the chattering of a few puffins; then as they watched and listened, more puffins came swooping right into holes on the side of the tall sand cliffs.

"Wow, look at them, Lloyd! Every one of those guys are flying straight into a hole! Every one of them! How do those puffins do that?"

"Well, God made each puffin in a special way for them to be able to perform that stunt that's for sure. In each hole, there is one single egg inside. About this time, some of them have probably hatched. These little guys mate for life."

"What does that mean, *mate for life*?"

"That means each boy and girl puffin stay with each other until they die. The normal life span is between twenty to twenty-five years. They like to eat small fish. Do you know why we are lucky today?"

Parker thought for a moment and then replied, "Because we are spending the day together, and maybe you and mommy will be together for life too?"

"Hmm...that is a wonderful thought, Parker. I certainly have dreamed about that very thing...many times, my friend. So, let me tell you about these puffins. They spend nearly all their life out on the ocean. They swim a lot, but when they need a rest, they can float on the waves. When they want to catch a fish, they swim under water to get them for their meal. It is only when they breed, meaning making an egg, will they return to cliffs like these."

Parker realized how special this was and said, "Lloyd, are you and I best friends?"

Lloyd reached forward in the canoe a little and touched the back side of Parker's shoulder. "You are my best little friend."

Lloyd and Parker remained there a little longer to enjoy God's mastery. They then turned to go back into the inlet and away from the ocean water. On their return trip, they viewed some geese cruising overhead in a V shape pattern. Much lower in the sky was the occasional grouse flying into their nests.

"Now, Parker, see that wooded area to our right?"

"You mean, at about three o'clock?"

Lloyd chuckled while saying, "You are 100 percent right, Parker, about three o'clock! I am going to steer us over to that part of the inlet."

In a few minutes, they approached the area where Lloyd wanted to be.

"Let's rest our paddles again and see if we can view anything under the water."

A few fish swam by which delighted Parker. With a quiet voice, he asked if Lloyd had also seen them. A pair of mallard ducks paddled out from the submerged tree roots and seaweed. Then something silently rose to the surface and glided back into the murky depths.

"Dad, I mean Lloyd, sorry. Did you see what moved next to us? I looked a little too late to see."

"I think it was a wood turtle or a painted turtle, both of those are common around here. Let's wait and see if it comes back."

For several minutes, they waited in whispered silence. Then the same movement came back. This time, they both were looking just to the right side of the canoe and saw a huge turtle swimming by. Even though the moment was for just a few seconds, Lloyd and Parker got a great look at it.

"Wow, Lloyd! Did you see that guy? That turtle must have been the biggest one in God's whole world! What kind of turtle was he?"

Lloyd knew this particular guy lived here and was so pleased that he showed himself. Lloyd answered Parker and said, "I have named him Fred, I have seen him several times, once even while I was standing on the pier where we launched our canoe. He is a snapping turtle and weighs, I guess, about forty pounds, although some of these species can weigh up to seventy pounds. Maybe he will grow that big. The *Maine's Nature Guide Book* that I have says that some have been seen the size of a manhole cover."

"You mean, one of those turtles could be as large as one of those round metal things you sometimes see in the road? Wow!"

The buddies stayed there, hoping for another look, but Fred did not return to make an appearance. After a little more time for them to share, they carefully paddled the canoe out of the wooded area. Now paddling like pros, the two headed once again to the pier to disembark. Within a few short minutes, they reloaded the canoe in the truck bed and tied it down.

Once back into the front seats, Parker leaned over to Lloyd and gave him a sideways hug. Then he said, "Lloyd, we make a pretty good team, don't we?"

Not needing an answer, Parker started humming a little tune as Lloyd backed his truck out of the parking place. Both men were smiling all the way home.

CHAPTER
27

An Odd Plane Ride

While still in bed and under the covers, Klem took a peek at their clock radio on his nightstand. With his movement, Jane woke up and gazed at her husband. She would have loved to just lay there to admire the man she had shared forty-nine years of her life. But she needed to make sure they began their day. She softly said to Klem, "Good morning, dear. What time is it? I hope we did not oversleep since we need to get up at five."

Klem answered his wife just at the same time the radio clicked on to wake them. As they explained to Parker the day before, Klem was going to take Lloyd to the airport and Jane would stay at home with Parker. She told him that after breakfast, they would play a game or two of Scrabble. Jane was rather good at the word game, but Parker won as many times as she did.

So as not to wake Parker who was still sleeping, as quietly as possible, they washed up and got dressed. Again, as planned, Klem would wait on the front porch for Lloyd and then head right off to the Portland International Airport.

By six o'clock, Klem was heading outside with his coffee mug in his hand. A few minutes later, Lloyd arrived, parked his truck in the driveway, and joined Klem.

"I want to thank you for your willingness to take me to the airport…especially since it is so early in the morning. I appreciate this."

Klem finished his coffee by taking his last sip and said, "Your totally welcome, my good fellow. All I ask is that you bring Abby back safely and in one piece."

* * * * *

Lloyd found his way to the correct airline check-in and waited in line. He did not have to give his baggage to the lady, he would be carrying it with him. While waiting in line, he looked around and noticed most people were happy. There were single men and women, most likely traveling on business. Some couples were holding hands, and other young families had children in arms with older ones standing close to their mom and dad.

Gosh, he thought, *I pray that one day, I could be a dad with a family like these. I know with Abby sharing my life, it truly would be a blessing.*

The line moved along, and eventually, Lloyd went through the check-in process. He was directed to the seating areas where he and the other passengers would wait.

When the announcement was made that everyone could line up to board, he took his duffle bag and joined the rest. He expected to go through the door directly onto the plane, so he was surprised to be walking through a portable skyway.

At the end of the skyway, Lloyd nervously entered the plane. The flight attendant welcomed him, and then he headed to his assigned seat. Lloyd stood with others in single file to wait for the passengers in front of him to settle in. When he found the seat that corresponded to the number on his boarding pass, he reached up and stored his duffle bag in the overhead compartment as he saw everyone else do.

Just as he was ready to sit, a female voice behind him spoke. With a hand on his shoulder, the lady asked, "Hi there, tall, dark, and handsome! Would you be willing to help a damsel in distress with my carry-on bag?"

Lloyd turned around and, with a forced smile on his face, took her bag and placed it next to his in the overhead. She thanked him profusely and slid past him to her window seat. Lloyd thought she really did not have to touch the side of his shoulder to keep her balance but figured she was just being friendly.

Because of Lloyd's horrible fear of heights, Jane had suggested that he might ask Dr. Lowell if she would give him a small relaxing pill to help him with his flight. Lloyd appreciated her caring suggestion but decided to *man it up,* as they say, and also grin and bear it.

He exhaled a large, nervous breath and took a writing pad from his top pocket and a mechanical pencil. He figured if everything was quiet on the plane, he could draw up some plans for his next wood project. Concentrating on the design and amount of lumber needed, he pretended that he was sitting safely at his kitchen table.

A while back, when Lloyd took Parker to see his gazebo construction, it was the ingenious scaffolding that Lloyd was most proud of. Even though the scaffolding that he put together was strong and secure and safe, it still took him a while to even get used to fifteen or twenty feet off the ground.

At this point, he didn't want to even think about how high above mother earth this airplane would be traveling. Sitting in his coach seat and trying to convince himself, he thought, *Okay, Lloyd, you can do it, concentrate on this wood project.* Silence would be golden for him. Then as fate would have it, the flight attendant appeared from somewhere and stood in the plane's aisle. She had a pleasant smile and was ready to start some kind of announcement.

"Welcome to Star Airlines. Now that everyone has found your assigned seats, please securely fasten your safety belts, and place your seats in the full upright position. In the slot in front you, you will find our plane's safety card. Please familiarize yourselves with the locations of the two emergency exits on both ends of the cabin."

She pleasantly pointed to the emergency exits in front of her, then those behind her.

"In the unlikely case of a water emergency landing, your seat cushion can be used as a floatation devise by pulling it forward and upward. Place your arms through the handles like this."

She used her prop to show the proper action. By this time in her informational presentation, Lloyd thought it *couldn't possibly* get worse. Then with a corporate kind of smile, the flight attendant continued, "If there is a sudden lack of air pressure, masks will come down from above your heads. Pull on the attached tube lightly to activate the air, and place it over your mouth like this."

Again, she used her prop to show how to do it correctly.

"If there is a child sitting near you, first activate yours then help them with theirs."

Lloyd swallowed hard a few nervous times and closed his eyes.

"We should be taxing shortly and receiving our communication from the tower to head to New York City with our nonstop flight. The duration of our flight is two hours and ten minutes and will be flying at an altitude of fifteen thousand feet. On behalf of myself, our cabin staff, and our pilots, we would like to thank you for choosing Star Airlines. We hope that you will think of us for your future traveling plans."

By the end of her presentation that seemed to be an endless attack on his nerves, Lloyd was almost fit to be hit over his head. His hands were shaking in time with the pounding beat of his heart.

After these distractions, Lloyd wandered back into his thoughts. His mind went into wondering what was in store for him. Will the woman of his dreams still have that same attraction for him and their incredible love affair? God, he sure hoped and prayed that their love would endure. If he lost her, he would feel that half of his soul would wither away and die.

He looked at his hands and noticed that he was clenching his armrests on his chair tightly. He released his grip and rubbed his hands together a few times and then placed them on either side of his body. As soon as he did that, he felt the air cabin pressure increase and heard the whirl of the jet engines as the plane lifted from the runway.

* * * * *

By this time, the lady next to him could see Lloyd's nervous distress. She decided that it was time for her to talk.

"Now don't worry about a thing. Flying is safer than walking across a Manhattan street in uptown New York City. You will be fine, trust me. Would you like me to pull down the window shade?"

While she maneuvered the shade, she overexaggerated her movements in a way that she thought her feminine attraction would be noticed.

"So, my seat partner, is that better? I don't think I caught your name. My name is Goldie. What may your name be?"

She offered her hand, and Lloyd pulled his hand from between the seat to meet hers. Instead of a handshake, she tried to sooth him by cupping his hand between both of her overtanned hands.

Lloyd managed to not notice her forwardness and said, "Nice to meet you, Goldie, my name is Lloyd."

For a fifty-or-so-year-old woman, Goldie was not unpleasant for a man to view. When she wore her clothes rather tight and a size too small, many men passing on the street would turn their attention to look at her a little longer than in a casual way.

To keep her looks, Goldie thought that wearing a little more jewelry added attractiveness to her overall appearance although she never asked any male.

"So, Lloyd, I might have seen you drawing. I suspect that you are an artist. I love artists. They have more techniques than most men…if you know what I mean. I see the artistry in your hands, your face, your soul."

Lloyd could not believe the forwardness of this lady. He did however feel the need to correct her.

"Goldie, I am not an artist. I am in construction. I am a woodworker. I build decks, porches, sheds, gazebos."

Goldie put on an "I am so interested" expression and said, "Oh gazebos, I love those little things. They are so cute. They are like… hmm…now don't tell me…oh yes they are used for outhouses. I knew it. How interesting!"

Lloyd decided it was not worth it for him to correct her. Besides, before he had a chance to say anything, she continued her monologue.

"Well, I haven't told you anything about me, no apologies needed, my plane partner. When growing up as a college student, I was never able to go to spring break like all my girlfriends. I just had to stay home during my whole vacation. Can you imagine, a sweet girl like me staying home for two whole weeks with my parents?"

She looked at Lloyd a little too long with a little hurt puppy dog look in her eyes. She was good at that. She lifted her right arm and placed it on Lloyd's as if needing his undivided sympathy.

"So I married a man who, I think, loves his job more than little old, I mean, *young* me. Can you believe that he would not leave his office to go to Long Island with me? I mean, he would have a whole week with me. But no…I guess I know that I place a far second in his life."

Lloyd was hoping for another announcement from the flight attendant to break up her almost one-sided conversation.

"So I was just sitting here thinking that you might like to share my one-bedroom West Hampton timeshare. We could have a lot of fun frolicking in the surf and such. I would let you rub suntan oil on me…to protect my soft delicate skin."

Lloyd leaned into the aisle to see where the restrooms were located. He thought that maybe he could spend some time in there to get away from Goldie. But to his surprise, the flight attendant started her well-rehearsed spiel to prepare passengers for the descent into JFK airport.

When the jet landed and taxied to the enclosed passenger walkway, Lloyd decided that he wanted to wait for everyone on the plane to find their belongings and proceed to the front of the plane. Goldie was fetching for something in her pocketbook. At first, she seemed to have control over herself, almost elegantly. Then her act of looking in her purse evolved into simple desperation. Finally, she finished her mission and regained Lloyd's hand.

"Lloyd, dear, here is my cellphone number and address of my timeshare. I hope you can make it, big guy! Remember one whole week with me!"

She pushed her hastily written note in Lloyd's top shirt pocket, tapping it with her hand. As a gentleman, a very naive gentleman, he said, "Very nice meeting you...ugh...Goldie."

As he unclipped his seat belt and retrieved both of their pieces of luggage, Goldie tried one more time and responded, with a seductive flare, "Lloyd, dear, you have no idea how very nice it could be!"

As he allowed Goldie to go in front of him, his own reality came back. Walking down the plane's narrow aisle, he continued onward to his uncertain destiny.

CHAPTER
28

New York City for Two

Sometime before the first passenger left the plane, the flight attendant stationed herself by the exit door, next to the cockpit. As Lloyd passed by her, with a nice smile, she wished him a pleasant visit to New York City. He thanked her and stepped onto the skywalk to the airport lobby. He took Goldie's note and placed it in the skywalk trash can. Looking forward, he felt that it was so good to be walking on solid floors again.

With a total rush of excitement and adrenalin, Lloyd caught a glimpse of Abby's smiling face as passengers hurried past her. His whole body shuttered with joy as they both ran to each other. In their embrace, it seemed that there was no one else around in the entire world.

Lloyd was first to ask, "How are you, my love? Even though we have been apart only a few days, I missed you so much, darling."

"Oh, Lloyd, I have been really busy, but I also missed you like crazy! Well…things are good. My college friend and her roommate are something else. They both welcomed me to their apartment, and Terri helped me so much with work contacts. Honey, I need to tell you what I am thinking about with all this New York City relocating and my career. But first, let's find the bus shuttle to get out of here."

The overhead digital signs in the airport greatly helped them find the way to the shuttles on the outside lane. Every twenty or so minutes, a new shuttle arrived to pick up commuters and take them downtown. Still holding hands, they waited on the loading platform area for the next one to arrive.

Within minutes, another one came up, stopped, and the driver opened the doors. It was sparsely filled, so they had their choice of places to sit. After selecting a seat, they snuggled in with each other.

At the airport, Abby had briefly told Lloyd about her last three days but wanted to hear about his.

"So what have you been doing, my love? How was your airplane trip? Were you terrified?"

"Oh, I have been crazy at work. Dr. Doris Lowell and her husband, Sam, invited me to have dinner when I was working on their patio. They are such a nice couple and are very happy with the construction progress. Yesterday, I took Parker on a canoeing trip out on Big Duck Inlet. He and I had a wonderful time. Of course, he misses you, but that special afternoon together helped us both. We saw Fred, the huge snapping turtle that I have seen a few times on other occasions. Parker will probably want to tell you about it, so don't let him know I told you.

"My fear of heights and flying? Well, that has not changed, and I am glad that you and I are going back to Port James on the train. Much closer to the ground! So…what can I say about the flight? Hmm…let me just say that I was extremely grateful when we landed, and that was for more than one reason."

One of the shuttle stops was Grand Central Station, but they stayed on to go to Rockefeller Plaza. When they got off the shuttle bus, Lloyd stepped away a few feet then just lingered, looking up in total amazement.

"Just look at those skyscrapers, I can't believe it! Goodness! There are so many more than I have ever imagined."

Abby had to chuckle at Lloyd's first reaction to the Big Apple.

"I know how you feel, my man from his little town. I had the very same reaction, and I did exactly what you have just done. Isn't it totally unbelievable? Now, we can't stay here forever looking up like typical small-town tourists."

Abby took out a white folded piece of paper from her pocket-book and started to read silently. Turning around to get her bearings, she said, "Nancy and Terri gave me a list of some things we could do today. Gosh, Terri jotted down so many wonderful things to see and visit. Let's see, for one day, we probably won't have nearly enough time for most of these. We definitely will need to prioritize. Montauk Point lighthouse would be simply delightful, but it is located way out at the tip of Long Island. Unfortunately, that would be a whole day trip for us.

"Here in the city is Radio City Music Hall and the world renowned Rockettes. Lloyd, you would love to see them do their famous leg kick, all perfectly synchronized in a row! We should also visit the World Trade Center Memorial. There are both indoor and outdoor narrated tours. Oh! Of course, over on West 3rd Street and 5th Avenue is the Empire State Building. Terri writes that it is 1,454 feet high and has some interactive museum floors. She says that the view from the top is simply breathtaking. Okay. First let's head over to those cluster of tents. For some reason, they listed this place on the paper that she wrote for us."

Lloyd thought that even to walk across from one side of the sidewalk to the other was a challenge in itself. He felt that looking at the crowded pace of endless pedestrians, he could have used a turning signal.

The fifteen or so pleasantly arranged tents were used for vendors. It reminded both of them of Port James's seasonal arts and crafts fair. Each small tent had different kinds of merchandise to sell. One had scarfs, gloves, hats, and accessories of all kinds. Another had dress boots and stockings, while a few had snacks such as candy, bags of peanuts, and energy bars. It was interesting to Lloyd how nicely each vendor presented their wares, especially the one with artwork paintings.

When they approached a souvenir tent, Abby said they had to go in so she could buy something for Parker. Picking up various trinkets, she found a small model of the Empire State Building, another was the Statue of Liberty. Holding one in each hand so Lloyd could see, she said, "Lloyd, which one do you think I should get for Parker? This one of the building or this other one of Old Liberty?"

Lloyd looked at both and said, "I'll buy one, and if you want, why don't you buy the other? He probably would like both."

They looked in several more vendor tents, enjoying the small-town feeling in the center of a huge city. Standing outside the last tent that sold various timepieces, they decided to look again at their list for a place to eat. With both of them sharing the paper, Abby said, "It says here that we should go to Third and Broadway to eat at Nathan's. She also has listed here several restaurants, but besides being expensive, it would unnecessarily use a lot of our afternoon. The nearest Nathan's is located at 40th Street and 6th Avenue."

They found the famous cart rather easily. The closer they were, the more often they saw New Yorkers holding their lunch in their hand. Most were eating the hot dog from a wrapped wax paper in one hand and a briefcase in the other. After waiting for a few customers to be served, they walked up to the cart window.

The nice man at Nathan's waited for them to make a decision. Without pausing, he instinctively took out two hot dogs from the hot water with his pair of metal tongs. Placing each of them in a fresh roll, with the wax paper around it, he said, "Hey, friends, I am Tony. What can I help you with today? A world-famous hot dog? First, the lady. What would you like?"

"Hi, Tony. I'll have a hot dog with a little sweet relish and ketchup."

Tony dipped his spatula into the relish and placed a thin layer on her order. Squeezing the ketchup from a bottle, he gave it to Abby and then asked what Lloyd would like. Lloyd decided to have sauerkraut and a small squirt of mustard on his.

Handing them through the cart window, Tony asked, "Anything else? I have Lay's chips, cheese Doritos, Cape Cod chips, Cheetos, Ruffles, and Fritos. Of course, I have my giant New York style dill pickles, the best-tasting pickles anywhere in this fine city! We are famous for them as well as our hot dogs."

Abby said she was okay with just the hot dog. Lloyd answered that he would have the Cape Cod chips and one of his dill pickles. Tony responded, "For your chips, I have classic, salt and vinegar and barbecue. How about drinks?"

Abby asked for a bottled water, and Lloyd had a Cherry Coke. Tony gave them their change and said, "Now that we are friends, come back to see me. Okay? I am here year-round for your ultimate eating pleasure."

Some of the people around the vendor truck chuckled a little to themselves. It seems that they all love Tony's personality. Abby and Lloyd turned around and found a convenient park bench where they could watch people going by. The hot dogs were the best they tasted, but maybe it was because they were so hungry.

After disposing of their wax paper and bottles in the nearest trash can, Abby said, "Darling, I would just love to go to one of New York's finest department stores. I don't care if we go to Lord and Taylor, Macy's, Saks, or whatever. Let's just head to Fifth Avenue and see what we find."

As they walked along, Lloyd could not believe how artistically presented each store window display was. It must have taken weeks to do each one. He had only seen such things this nice in movies.

Before long, they were being gently pushed through the revolving doors of a famous and treasured downtown department store. Now inside, they were bathed with a wonderful visual delight. They looked around and watched the hustle of shoppers *dressed to the tea*, all carrying named brand store shopping bags. Just for the fun of it, they walked to the center of the department store to find the escalators. They took the moving stairs to every level, pausing only to get the flavor of each until they arrived at women's shoes.

"Lloyd, let's check out the shoes here, maybe I will get a pair or even two."

As they walked from the escalator, Abby's eyes feasted on artistically presented shoes on clear glass backlit shelves. The shelves were lined along the wall of a beautifully carpeted display room. It struck Lloyd as elegant, with an ultramodern appearance. In the center of the showroom stood a well-dressed male employee. He wore his apparel flawlessly, which worked perfectly with his nicely groomed haircut. Abby casually looked around as the man waited for the best time to ask if she needed any help with her selection.

Nonchalantly, Abby picked up one *diamond* studded high heel with a designer logo on the side. She was instantly attracted to its style and sultry look. Since there was no price on the gem, she took the shoe to the salesman. He said, "Yes, that delish pair is from Christian Louboutin of Italy. Let me look at my price list. What size do you take?" Abby told him either a 6 1/2 or 7.

He asked, "Would that be an American or European size, madam?"

"Abby said, I guess American."

While waiting for him to tell the price, she turned the high heel around a few times, examining its perfect stitching and graceful shape.

"Well, we do have it in your size. You would look and feel absolutely stunning. It is $3,500, without tax. Would you like to try this one or any others in my designer collection?

CHAPTER
29

A Serious Talk and a Harbor Cruise

It did not take long for Lloyd and Abby to quickly excuse themselves from the upscale designer shoe area and head back onto the busy city street. After another look at their little folded paper, they decided to walk to 7th and 42nd Street. When they arrived there, Abby said, "Take a good look at this intersection, Lloyd. Does it look familiar to you at all?"

Lloyd thought that was a senseless question since he had never been even close to New York City. Then, realizing this intersection was Times Square, he almost shouted, "I can't believe my eyes, Abby! This is where on New Year's Eve, that huge silver ball drops at the stroke of midnight! Wow! I have watched it on television every year since I was ten years old!"

Abby adored his delight in actually standing there. It truly was a special place where the New Yorkers celebrated, the tradition going back years. Terri had shown her this spot during her tour three days ago. She allowed a few minutes for Lloyd to have this ambiance sink in; then, she said, "Our next thing to do is head west about five blocks on 42nd Street. We need to find Pier 83 where the Circle Line Tour ships depart. I don't think that we need to take a bus, it should not take more than ten minutes or so to walk."

Since the weather was perfect, walking was a pleasure; besides, it was fun to look at everything on the way.

"You know, Lloyd, we are so close to the Broadway Theater District. We just have to take a detour up three blocks north of here."

The two of them could not believe the numerous famous theaters. They went past only a fraction of them. As they walked past, they saw the fronts of the Lyceum Theater, Marquis Theater, The Palace, Richard Rodgers, and the Majestic Theater. Lloyd was especially excited to see the outside of the Saint James Theater.

He remembered his parents telling him about when they attended school in Port James. All through grade school and then in high school, they were classmates. For their senior class trip, the students went there to see Carol Channing in *Hello Dolly!* He believed that it must have been in the year 1965.

After this short detour through part of the Theater District, they crossed the street and walked up to the ticket booth on Pier 83. The man at the ticket booth for the Circle Line Tour told them that the next ship would be leaving shortly at 5:00 p.m. He printed up two tickets and took Lloyd's payment of $88. He told them that the guided tour was for the two and a half hours around part of New York Harbor. After receiving their two tickets, they found the place where white benches were exclusively reserved for the customers to wait.

Sitting here at the harbor was so fascinating to Lloyd. On the water, cargo ships pulled their products, both raw material and finished items, from all over the world. Behind them, the sound of the city streets from cars and trucks traveling in all directions added to the city's dynamic life. Owning the sky, jet airplanes were cutting through the atmosphere; there was life all around. Everything they experienced seemed to be constantly moving quickly to their destination.

Eventually, they saw their boat coming into view as it passed by some larger ships that were docked. With the help of the small crew, it pulled into the pier only a few hundred feet from their seating area. The man in the ticket booth asked everyone to form a line while the previous tourists walked off the ship and down the short gangplank onto the pier.

Within a few short minutes, Lloyd and Abby were on the lower deck deciding where they wanted to stay for the tour. Abby asked if they could go up the stairs to the outside top deck so they could see all around them. She also wanted to view the gulls and smell the salt water that reminded her of home. Most importantly, she wanted to find a place away from other tourists with their children running around excitedly. Her plan was to talk to Lloyd while cruising around the harbor. She thought there would be enough time between the narrations from the ships' loud speaker.

As the ropes were untied and the ends thrown onto the ship, they felt the diesel engines start the props to move the vessel. Over the sound system, the captain welcomed everyone and then introduced the announcer and what they would be viewing.

While cruising around the harbor, they heard a woman's voice briefly describing points of interest. The voice spoke of American history with interesting facts about Ellis Island, One World Trade Center Memorial, Manhattan's skyline, the Statue of Liberty, and then the New Jersey's skyline.

Abby thought that she might have missed her own opportunity for her necessary talk with Lloyd, but during the return trip, the tour guide allowed the passengers to just enjoy cruising on the water without any more messages.

As they passed the Statue of Liberty once again, she knew they would be out on the water for forty-five minutes or more. It was truly a beautiful day with a slight warm breeze and almost a pure blue sky overhead.

"My darling Lloyd, you are the most cherished and perfect blessing that God has ever wanted to give a woman. I don't know why, but I am so glad that my heavenly Father has chosen me to have you, but He has. I thank Him every day, *every day, my dearest!*"

Lloyd was looking into her ocean blue eyes, and Abby returned his caring, loving, expression as she held his hand tight, adoring his gorgeous big brown eyes.

"My love, as you know, I needed to come here after I received Terri's letter that she sent to me. Living in New York City, there are so many numerous benefits that this awesome city offers, but there are many negative aspects. As I have seen firsthand, those things were very extreme and personally appalling for me to accept."

"What I could not live with is not having you in my life to share every day. Lloyd, I would never consider living here without you."

Lloyd looked at their hands holding on to each other and said nothing for a while. Abby knew that he needed this pause and lovingly waited for him to say something.

"Abby, you know that I love you, and I would follow your dreams whatever they are. I love my enchanting little village and the sea-swept coast of Port James. However, besides you and Parker, Klem and Jane, and a few friends, there is no one else there for me. Of course, Parker would be coming with us. But living here, could I be totally happy? What would happen to me and my love of working in wood? From what I can see, the whole city and area is made of concrete, steel, and glass. What would I do for work? How could I support you and Parker?"

"Lloyd, I understand fully and completely what you are saying. Darling, before I continue, please hug me for a few minutes."

There on the deck, two lovers held each other among both God's creation and man's creation. Abby felt Lloyd's warmth and tender hold. She could have stayed in his embrace forever, but she needed to continue.

"I must tell you some more, love. During my short trip to this city, I learned that the receptionist at the magazine is married to a woodworker. They live in Brooklyn, just on the other side of the East River from Manhattan. She commutes an hour or more each way to work at *New York Trend Magazine*. See, her husband has more than enough work, building wonderful projects like you have done. They are really happy in Brooklyn, but he is planning to slow down a little fairly soon. From what Terri has told me, he has not started looking but will soon want a helper, or even a full partner. Eventually, the position could lead to taking over the business that he developed over the years."

This was so much for Lloyd to take in, but he tried to make sense of it all. His mind was whirling.

"Abby, I never thought that could be possible, but it just might work. I should talk with this man, maybe meet with him face-to-face. If this is what you want, before we do anything more, we should check out this Brooklyn area. Abby, we both want the best for Parker too. Are there good middle schools there for him? This would be such a harsh change for the little guy."

"Oh, I know, I truly have thought about that too. I have to believe that Parker would adjust as long as he has both of us in his life…I think. Maybe at first, we would need to move to Greenwich Village for a short time until we get organized.

"The supervisor at the magazine has an opening in the travel section. He is kind of odd, but both Nancy and Terri seem to be able to put up with him. So…instead of a formal interview, he asked me for a sample of my writing skills. I have already sent him an e-mail with a sample of my work."

The ship was closing in a little closer to the New York skyline. This was becoming the end of their trip, but the beginning of their lives.

"Abby, I really need to have some time for all of this to sink in my head. It is pretty clear, however, that we would have to make a few more visits here, including visiting Greenwich Village as well as Brooklyn. As I said before, I would also need to talk with that receptionist's husband. No matter what, it would be interesting to talk with a fellow woodworker."

"Lloyd, do you still love me?"

"Yes, with all my heart."

As that exchange was given, the ship moved along the side of the pier, finishing the trip.

30

Getting In

The two lovers found a little cozy restaurant near the docks to eat some late dinner. They were more exhausted than hungry because of the nervousness that they carried in their stomachs. The food was good, and they managed to eat with a coming appetite.

As they sat inside by the restaurant's front window, Abby and Lloyd saw the complexion of the outside street activity change. Earlier in the day, pedestrians were either businesspeople, shoppers, or out-of-town tourists. Now that it was later in the evening, the city's activities gave way to patrons of restaurants and upscale dance clubs and bars.

After a few more minutes of street watching, they finished their dinner and paid the bill. Back out on the street, they decided to flag a taxi and took the ride to Nancy and Terri's apartment. It was only a fifteen-minute taxi ride to her place. After getting out of the cab and while walking up to the apartment's façade, they realized the hour was quite late. Taking the elevator to the third floor, they walked the hallway to their door. Abby used her key and opened it as quietly as possible.

Nancy had already enjoyed a glass of wine and went to bed while Terri was working on her computer at the kitchen table. As soon as they came in, Terri closed her laptop and walked over to give Lloyd a little hug.

"So, girlfriend, this must be Lloyd. At least I hope it is. Otherwise, I just hugged a total stranger that came through my door! Lloyd, I have heard nonstop about so many wonderful things concerning you. That is reassuring because Abby has been my best friend for more than four years."

Lloyd pulled his small duffle bag off his back and placed it down. Terri turned to Abby and gave her a warm hug and a kiss on her cheek. When they stepped away from each other, she said, "As you can see, I made up the couch into the guest bed for you, Lloyd. I hope it is comfortable. It came with the apartment along with the rest of the furniture we use here. I never slept in it, but it seems okay."

By this time, Lloyd was so tired, he could have slept on a rock. Abby went to get a drink of water and offered some to Lloyd. Taking the glass, he said, "Thanks, darling, I should have gotten a glass for you. Say, Terri, my gal here certainly knows her way around town. You must have taught her well with your crash course."

The three of them talked a little more about Nathan's, window shopping, and the Circle Line ship tour. Finally they all decided it was time to call it a night. After each of them used the bathroom, they went to their separate rooms and crawled into bed.

CHAPTER
31

Daybreak

Morning came soon, but the sun was still hidden behind the nearby buildings. Both Nancy and Terri tiptoed around so Abby and Lloyd could sleep a little longer.

By the time the sun found its way into the living room window, they had already left for the day. Terri had some breakfast rolls on a plate for them and left a message on a piece of paper next to the rolls.

Abby awoke and, after showering, came into the living room. By this time, Lloyd had remade the bed into the couch and had already washed up and shaved. She saw Lloyd sitting on the couch and looking at his smartphone, so she went over to him.

"Hi, *soul mate*, how did my man sleep last night?" She gave him a morning hug and went to the kitchen table.

"Wow, Abby, you never called me that before. Have you elevated my status? Don't get me wrong, that sounds so nice."

"Well, my man, you are certainly on the top of my list." With a smile on her face, she noticed the note that Terri wrote to her. She sat down and read it.

My dear friend,

It truly was wonderful to have spent some time with you. I wish you had been able to visit a little longer. My work always seems to take so much of my free time.

I know that you have so much to think about, I remember how it was for me. No matter what you decide, please know that you will always be my best friend. Please keep in touch, especially whenever you make a decision.

Now, I have one question for you. Where did you find that dreamy man of yours? Does he have a twin brother? Let me know if he does. I want pictures and his e-mail address, okay?

Seriously, I hope you make the right decision for yourself. And remember, I love you, roommate.

Your best friend, Terri,
Many hugs to you!

Abby placed Terri's letter down and touched it a few times with her fingertips. Then she carefully placed it in her luggage, which was standing next to her. She looked at her watch and said, "Honey, we better take off to the station. It would be terrible if we missed the train."

With one last look around to make sure neither of them left anything behind, Abby placed the apartment key on the table, and they went into the hallway. There was a sign on the elevator that said it was out of order, so they took the steps down the three stories and stepped outside. Abby took one last look up at her friend's window and then slid the handle out of her luggage to prepare for toting behind.

Lloyd started to unfold his city map to figure which way to go, but Abby said, "We will need to cross the street to get the 6th Avenue bus, going northbound. We take that bus for forty blocks to Bryant

Park on 42nd Street. Then we will get off and walk east for three blocks to Park Avenue. Grand Central Terminal should be on our left. So, honey, lets cross here."

To say the least, Lloyd could not believe Abby knew her way around like that. Once they were across the street and waiting at the bus stop sign, he said that he was very impressed.

"Oh, it's not that hard to navigate. Avenues run north and south, streets run east and west. For any address, you always say the street first, then the avenue. Streets are either east or west, from, I think, 5th avenue...you will get the idea."

When the bus came, a few people got out from the center doors, giving Abby and Lloyd just enough room to board but not to sit. As the bus traveled along, if no one was waiting at the outside bus stop, the driver passed it without stopping. When a passenger needed to get off the bus at the next stop, they pulled a cord located up along the inside wall. Hearing the bell, the driver became aware that he needed to let them off. It always worked perfectly.

All this was so new to Lloyd, and he was amazed but had a lump in his throat thinking of ever leaving Port James that he grew to love so dearly. He looked at Abby who was measuring their progress by bending down every so often to look out the bus window. After her last visual check, she pulled the cord, and the two of them maneuvered to the middle door to leave.

Once outside, they walked the few remaining city blocks and entered Grand Central Station. The interior totally stunned Lloyd. He slowed his gait and tried to take it all in. Abby saw his action and said, "Honey, we need to keep up our quick pace. We have to get to track number 9 where it says Departures, see it way down there?"

Again, Lloyd was impressed with his love who gave him the thought that she could manage the city with no problem. He just couldn't help but feel that this whole thing could result in putting a lot of stress on their relationship. Maybe he just had to rely on God to help both of them make it through the next few months or more. Lloyd would pray tonight to earnestly ask for extra divine help for each of their life steps.

CHAPTER 32

Train Ride

As the passenger train slowly pulled out of the station, Abby gazed out their train window to look one more time at the impressive New York City skyline. The late afternoon sun reflected off thousands and thousands of building windows.

To Abby's own surprise, she had a tear in her eye. She tried to decide whether it was saying goodbye to the exciting pace of the Big Apple or already missing her girlfriend. For whatever the reason, she suddenly felt extremely tired. After such an exhausting few days, the gentle rocking of the train as it sped along its tracks felt soothing to her.

Lloyd was feeling the same drain of energy. In fact, after settling in their comfortable seats, both of them took a well-deserved nap.

Several hours of their sleep melted away like it was only a minute. As what can happen from time to time on a train ride, a sudden jolt woke them from their rest. They both reacted by reaching for each other's hand, then smiled. Lloyd released her hand and reached his arms over this head for a satisfying stretch. He said to Abby, "I'll need to make some more sketches and write up cost estimates for a few upcoming customers in Port James. The Coopers want a cupula for their garage roof. They want it to be lit from the inside. Then the Franks want a gazebo to be located off the front of their home on the left as viewed from the street. So if you don't mind, this would be a perfect time to draw a few more of those things. This way, I can review them with those people as soon as we get back to Port James."

"Well, love, I have some things to do too. First, I want to e-mail Terri to thank them for my visit. Then I think I will do some creative writing as an exercise just for myself."

So the time spent while traveling on the train to Port James would serve the purpose. Abby got out her computer and started to compose.

Dear Terri,

> *How can I thank you enough? It was so special spending time with my super best and only college roommate. Honestly, taking me on a nice tour when you met me at Grand Central, seeing your apartment, and reminiscing good times was priceless.*
>
> *Advocating for me about the journalist position for your magazine was so precious of you... and such a temptation to jump right in. I so much appreciate you being patient with me. I promise to you that within this next week, I will make my decision. My dear, you are the best, and I am so pleased that you are happy.*
>
> *Please thank Nancy for letting me bunk in your charming apartment; that was so sweet of her. I am also happy that the two of you seem to hit it off so well. That is very special.*
>
> *God bless you, until later, your friend, Abby*

After reading through it one more time, Abby sent it off and began her next writing. She decided to write about two subjects as if they were the next articles for the magazine. Abby titled the first one "Walking Greenwich Village." It was a nicely formulated and informational piece, with a personal insight. The second was titled "The Sport of Sailing."

When she finished both articles, she felt that it read like a special submission to her diary book. She was proud of them both but felt the one about the Portland Observatory that she sent to Mr. Gram was the best of the three. She couldn't help but wonder if that meant anything.

The rest of the train trip was pleasant enough. Around dinnertime, they went to the dining car to have a bite to eat. Traveling a mile a minute, the train gave them the opportunity to watch outside scenes through its windows. Fleeting past them were brief and varied sights of humankind. Small towns and villages were scattered around farmlands. Others were separated by fields or wooded areas all flying by in seconds. Abby and Lloyd both had the same thoughts. People living with so many different lifestyles and communities probably love where they have called their home. For Abby, maybe that was a lesson that she was learning.

* * * * *

As the countryside scenes continued to flow past them through the train window, Abby turned to Lloyd and asked, "Say there, my love. If I see your sketches for your customers, I will let you read my articles."

Lloyd exchanged his sketches with her writings. He loved how her breath quickened as she looked at his work. It wasn't something controllable; it was just her natural excitement for his woodworking talent.

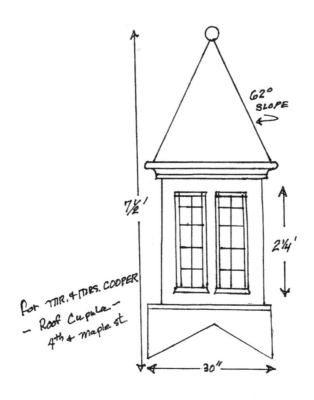

62°
SLOPE

7½'

2¼'

For MR. & MRS. COOPER
— Roof Cupola —
4th & Maple St.

30"

SKETCH FOR
MR. & MRS. FRANK
@ 3rd & Oak Avenue

The train slowed down to find its way to the little depot of Port James. Klem was waiting for the two people whom he loved so much to come down the train steps. A few other people were in front of them, then they appeared. Klem welcomed Abby and Lloyd with a hug; then, they walked to the parking lot behind the train depot. As he unlocked the car doors, he explained, "Jane wanted to be here to greet you, but of course, she needed to stay home with Parker. That little boy wanted to stay up to see you both but finally fell asleep on the couch next to her. I think that was around eleven o'clock. Jane got him into his bed and stayed up a little longer. While on the couch, she was catching up on some reading, but then, she also fell asleep. As I was getting my hat and coat, I told her that she should retire to the bedroom, and I would take off to get you. With a sleepy gaze, she agreed and went upstairs. So how was your trip? How was that crazy city? How is Terri doing?"

They managed to answer his questions as fully as they could. It was only after ten minutes that they were driving up to Klem and Jane's captivating little home. The Port James lighthouse was beaming its beautiful light as it traveled on its predetermined circular pathway.

After a few more sleepy pleasantries, Abby headed upstairs to her childhood bedroom. After checking on her sleeping son in the bedroom next to hers, she opened her own door and crawled into her bed. Lloyd was in the hallway, just behind her as he headed to the guest room.

They both fell asleep to the secure and safe sound of the lighthouse fog horn.

CHAPTER
33

Sunday Morning

Carrying her mug of Maine's Best brand of pumpkin spice–flavored coffee, Abby found her favorite spot on the front porch and nestled in "her" well-worn Adirondack chair. The fall air was crisp, making her hot coffee mug feel good on her fingers. In the cool air, her breath could be seen as she whispered thoughts to herself.

"Now I see why some people say that traveling is such an education. I truly care for my friendship with Terri, and I hope we can always have that. For the residents of that big city, there were such wonderful things…but to enjoy them, there were compromises that they all had to take. But Terri seemed to be able to handle them all…I think."

As if to bring her back to reality, the clear sound of church bells in the village started its hymn. Abby blinked a few times, took a sip of her coffee, and looked toward the sweet sound. They reminded her that over the short summer, she had not attended church even once. As concerned parents every Saturday night, Klem and Jane would ask if Abby would attend their church service the next day.

It seemed to Abby that there was always something else to do for her job search. She also felt the need and, more importantly, the desire to spend some quality time with Parker.

Thankfully, Parker was getting stronger, and the ailments from the Lyme disease were fading from his little body. For the last few months, Jane cooked with organic fresh fruits and vegetables to see if that kind of diet would help. She decided to prepare enough for the entire family. Jane thought that it couldn't hurt to give it a try, and after a while, she felt that it was making a difference.

Abby listened to the church hymn until the last bell was rung, then made her decision. This morning, she would go to church; it would be good for her. First, she needed to get Parker up from bed, then invite Lloyd by texting. With a smile on her face, she thought how this would also please her folks.

* * * * *

The Watercrests and Lloyd sat comfortably in the first row of the sanctuary. In fact, they completely filled the entire pew. Remarkably, they all had made it to Grace Lutheran Church with even a few minutes to spare. In this small community church, Klem and Jane had been faithful members for nearly sixty years. In so many ways, they felt that this church was their second home.

Lloyd paged through the church service bulletin but was thinking about when he was twelve years old. He recalled his confirmation at Grace Lutheran about ten years ago. In fact, Abby was in that same confirmation class during the two years of instruction taught by the church vicar.

The sanctuary was somewhat plain, with cream stucco walls and dark painted pews. The altar was made of white marble with a gold cross in the center. On both sides of the nave, the rounded pane windows were clear, but in the balcony where the choir sang was a beautiful round rose window. It was donated by Martha Snyder in memory of her late husband. The installation was completed with a small ceremony, many years after the church building was finished in 1840.

After the last remaining communicants found their place, Pastor Wells entered from the side. Norma, the choir director and organist, introduced the first hymn, "I Put My Trust in Only Thee." The normal liturgy was spoken by Pastor Wells, followed by the appropriate responses from the congregation, then another hymn was sung. Just after the scriptures for the day were read, Pastor continued with his sermon.

He was wearing the traditional black-and-white liturgical collar, which was visible under his white vestments. Pastor looked around his little church and at the members. He looked up at the rose window in the balcony for a moment, then commenced, "May the words of my mouth and the meditation of our hearts be acceptable in Your sight, oh Lord, God Almighty. My dear friends, this Sunday, I will be starting this sermon a little different than I usually do. You see, yesterday, I had a few hours between hospital visits, so I decided to have lunch at home. As I parked my car in our driveway, I thought that I would stroll around the house to enjoy my wife's gardens. She spends a lot of her time with her shrubs and flowers. In fact, a few years ago, she entered a few of her homegrown plants in the Port James flower show. She won third place for her blue irises and second for her giant taupe-colored peace rose.

"As I was taking in the fruits of her labor, I noticed the red miniature rose bush in her side garden. The blossoms are less than the size of a quarter, just like its little leaves. This plant never grows taller than eight inches, but every spring, it displays itself for the entire summer. Neither of us add rose food to this little life. It grows each year on its own...or in truth, by God's plan. It asks for nothing but warmth, some rain from the sky, and the soil for its little roots. In many ways, it is lost in our garden, except from time to time, I pause by it and enjoy its little color. I felt a little ashamed that I have taken it for granted. So if you would please join me, I would like to offer up a prayer."

Bowing his head, along with his church members, Pastor prayed, "Thank You, God, for life, even this little one, which appears besides the more magnificent blossoms around our home. I think You put it there for a reason. You wanted us all to be reminded to be thankful... for everything that is good, no matter how small. Thank you for our lives, our friends and family, this church, its members, and our little, precious, sea coast village of Port James. Heavenly Father, we give thanks for *all* your creation and thank you for every breath we take. Above all else, thank you for Jesus in our lives. Amen."

He then raised his head and continued with his favorite Bible verse, "This is the day that the Lord has made, let us rejoice and be glad in it!"

Abby pondered Pastor's prayer in her heart. It seemed to speak to her while she struggled with her life decision. As her thoughts swirled around in her head, she came to wonder. Was this particular church service the way God was speaking to her through Pastor's sermon?

She reached over for Lloyd's loving hand and was comforted to realize that he was reaching for hers at the same time. He delivered three little squeezes to her hand, which they both understood to mean *I...love...you.*

CHAPTER
34

On the Way to the Carnival

Autumn in Port James was a time for nature to lace some spectacular maple leaf colors that were interspersed between the perpetual green of the conifers. Both residents and visitors alike took to driving along the coast and into the small towns to enjoy the peak color of the season.

Along with these pleasures was the yearly fireman's carnival, which stayed for three days and partly benefited the volunteer fireman's working budget. Families and out-of-towners happily gathered into their cars to make the trip to the magically recreated fairgrounds. Standing in line to purchase their tickets, both children and parents looked around, pointing to every ride, planning which to go on first. The smell of cotton candy and fried waffle cones were mixed with the tantalizing aroma of Italian sausages, hotdogs, hamburgers, and chicken.

Evening at the fair gave an enchanting display of colored lights, which outlined each exciting amusement ride. Some of the larger rides sent fairgoers speeding up to the top. Those who kept their eyes open could see blue, green, red, and yellow colors streaming from their ride and reflecting onto the ocean surf.

That was evening, but today was noon, and the second sunny day for the fair. The Watercrests were around their kitchen table and just finishing an organic salad that Jane had made. By plan, Abby had invited her Lloyd over for lunch so that she could ask him a favor.

Parker was just slurping the last of his milk and was just about ready to take his glass into the kitchen. He was nursing a little burp that was almost ready to express itself. Abby tried to remind him of his manners, but she didn't verbalize it fast enough. Klem was already in front of the kitchen sink, filling it with hot soapy water. When he heard Parker's burp, he jokingly said, "Oh my, it must be misty outside! I thought I just heard the fog horn."

Lloyd joined in the fun and said, "Hey, Parker, my man, I am going to give that burp a four out of five for the degree of difficulty and an eight out of ten for your delivery. So the group of professional judges gives your performance an average of nine. I am truly proud of you!"

With that, Jane rolled her eyes, and Abby tried to keep her composure as a respectable mom. Without success, she then hid her little smile behind her napkin. To change the subject, she addressed her man.

"Lloyd, my big hunk, I was wondering if you would be willing to take us to the fair this afternoon. You know, it is the carnival in town."

Jane pitched in before he had a chance to answer, "Oh you guys! You absolutely must go! I convinced my Klem to take me last evening, and we had such a great time. In fact, we met Sarah and Fred Landen. You know Sarah, she is the lady that conducts the monthly community meetings. She always seemed so proper, especially during the meetings, but we saw another side of her at the fair.

"She dragged Fred on all the rides, and the whole time she was on them, she was screaming her head off. On the roller coaster, when they were speeding downward, Fred *plumb lost his brown wig!* Sarah went into an uncontrollable laughter that could be heard throughout the whole place. Fred turned around in his seat to try to catch it, but the darn thing flew right past him. It flung in the air and hit squarely onto Oliver Teamore's face seating right behind them! You know that Oliver is such a highly proper older gentleman. Well...

Oliver couldn't remove Fred's wig from his face because he could not take his hands off the bar that was holding them in.

"Oh! It truly was funny as ever! When the coaster finally stopped, poor Oliver who was still 'wearing' the toupee, looked like a frightened squirrel. His buggy eyes were just peaking over the fur."

By this time, everyone was laughing hysterically, while Parker was trying to mimic Oliver's expression. After getting napkins to wipe their laughing tears and between a few last giggles, Abby managed to ask one more time.

"So, Lloyd, it sure sounds fun, will you take us please?"

Parker added his six-year-old plea by asking, "Please, Lloyd, please...pretty please?

Lloyd pulled away from his chair and said, "Of course! So let's get going! It is one o'clock now, and we can stay until five. At six o'clock, I have to meet the Wallers at their home to discuss and plan out a replacement for their old porch."

Parker sprang over to Lloyd and gave him a high five. Jane watched her boys do the ceremonial action then said, "Parker, get your new red jacket from the closet, the one with the hood. You never know how cool it might get in a few hours."

Parker opened the closet door and reached up enough to pull the coat from its wooden hanger. He had his new jacket in his hand and had closed the closet door so quickly that the cloths hanger was still swinging back and forth, making a clunking noise on the closed door.

By this time, Jane had gone to the kitchen, which gave Klem an ear to whisper into.

"I really love that grandson kid of ours. I am so happy that he is feeling a little more normal. He seems like he has regained a lot of his energy!"

A Quick Response

Before leaving for the fair, Abby quickly checked her laptop for any new e-mails that came to her. While sitting on the couch, she placed her computer on her lap and carefully started down the line of correspondences. She stopped at the e-mail from Mr. Gram. Her fingers froze in place without opening it. After trying to breathe a little more regularly again, she placed her cursor on the message and left-clicked on it. With anxiety, she decided to go ahead and read the message.

> *Hi there, pretty lady! I just finished your article on the Portland Observatory Tower. To put it bluntly, you knocked my socks off! You are just what I have been hoping for. I am arranging the housekeeping staff to clean up your new office, those girls do a good job. Let's start you out at 30k with quarterly increases of 10k each until reaching 60k. Drop me a line with your acceptance, and I will get the paperwork in line for you. If you can make that antiquated, boring tower seem interesting to our magazine readers, I can't wait to see what you can write about the great things around here. Bye-bye good looking!*

CHAPTER 36

The Carnival

The fair was in full force, and Parker could not be any more excited. He hopped out of Lloyd's truck, then impatiently waited to go altogether. Walking along, Parker was holding his mom's hand but almost pulling her like a little puppy on a leash. Abby stopped walking, placed herself in front of her son, and said, "Now, Parker, you need to stay with us at all times. We will be able to get to everything with the time we have here. You know, I just want you to be safe."

Parker nodded in agreement and said, "Yes…yes…I understand."

The three of them made a beeline to the lady in the white ticket booth that was in the center of all the activity. Adults were reaching into their pockets to take out their wallets or opening purses for the same reason. Eventually, it was their turn. The young ticket girl, named Daisy, innocently boasting a generous and sweet smile, looked at them and said, "My, what a handsome and beautiful family. What a treat for me to see families like you! My name is Daisy. Now, how can I help you? I am guessing that you would like some tickets. How many tickets would you want? They are a dollar each, but I always like to tell my customers that most of the rides need four or five tickets each. That way, no one is disappointed."

Abby was also in front of her ticket booth and standing to the left of Lloyd. She had the opportunity to read the options printed on the booth just above her window. After scanning the sign, Abby said, "Daisy, I see that instead of buying a pile of tickets, we can purchase a four-hour pass for one price. Maybe we should go that route instead. The ticket girl nodded in agreement.

"Yes, I was just going to recommend that, especially if four hours seems like enough time for you. We also have a full-day pass for ten dollars more. Since half the day is already over, your best bet is the four-hour one. Let's see, that is thirty dollars per adult and fifteen for children under thirteen years old. So your bargain for today is seventy-five dollars."

Daisy received Lloyd's money, then said, "Okay, folks, please place the back of your hand on my pass-through, and I will stamp them."

So after the three of them got their hands stamped, they stepped aside to make way for the next customers. Daisy looked out her window toward them and said, "Thank you very much, and have a great day!"

After putting back his wallet in his pants pocket, Lloyd bent down to Parker and asked him, "Now which ride would you like to go on first? It looks like the merry-go-round doesn't have a long line."

Parker looked around at all the rides and decided that his friend was right. Abby said, "Hey, gentlemen, don't I have a vote for this?"

Parker thought about that and said, "Sure you do, Mom, but let's go on the merry-go-round first!"

Abby rolled her eyes but knew this plan would serve her very well. She did not like the more wild rides, so this one and a few others would be *her cup of tea.* Of course, she wasn't quite sure about her son. Although they did not discuss this, but she hoped that maybe her Lloyd would go with Parker on those other rides. She would be happier to watch from ground level.

After the merry-go-round ride, they exited and went up to a giant slide to watch for a while. One after another, both kids and adults arranged the blankets to sit on, then started their slide down to a pile of wood chips.

"Mom, I think you can do this one, it's kind of high, but not real wild."

Abby looked at Parker and thought to herself, *Wow! My little six-year-old picked up on that. Somehow he figured out that I only like less wild rides. He is so precious and caring.*

"Okay, guys, I will give it a try."

They were handed a burlap blanket from the man and, with a pointing gesture, directed them to walk up the stairs to the top.

Once there, Abby knew she couldn't turn back and disappoint her men, so she placed the blanket down, and sat on it. Before she knew it, Lloyd gave her a starting push down the slide. She was determined to keep her eyes wide open, and she did just that. Of course, just until she landed in the soft pile of wood chips. With chips on her clothes and in her long black hair, she sat there momentarily and started to laugh.

Well, she thought, *that was fun!*

Parker arrived within a few seconds followed by Lloyd, both giving out tons of laughter and grins. Parker picked himself up and announced, "We should do this one more time!"

Since there was no line to wait in, they took advantage of their good timing and went for three more "rides."

Having climbed the stairs of the great yellow slide four times, the tasty aromas coming from the food trucks took their attention. They moseyed over to where several staff were hard at work making entrées. Each vendor had their particular expertise displayed with colorful banners. There was an Italian food truck, specializing in their homemade meatballs over elbow pasta and red tomato sauce. Next to that was a German truck serving hot dogs or knockwurst with sauerkraut and warm potato salad.

What caught Abby's attention was a truck having a blue and white stripped canvas awning. The name on its banner was *Fisherman Jack's Fresh Seafood.* The rugged-looking man inside was wearing a yellow slicker and wide brimmed hat. Because they lingered a few moments in front of his ordering window, he started his spiel.

"Hi there, land lovers, my name is Rusty, but you can call me Rusty."

The three of them looked at each other with puzzled expressions, but he quickly continued on, "So what can I get you today? I have fresh caught lobster that are in easy-to-eat chunks and glistening in real melted butter. I have three sized bowls. The small one is called *the Mermaid*, the middle size is called *the Skipper*, and the one for only the hardy appetites is called *Captain Nemo*.

"It doesn't get any better than that. I should tell you we also have delicious chilled lobster rolls that make your taste buds dance and chilled lobster salads, made-to-order. I also have my world-famous fried fish sandwiches that are made from monkfish. Customers say that my monkfish tastes similar to lobster. I personally don't see it, but my family says the same thing. Besides, like I say, those sandwiches of mine *are* world-famous. Oh! I almost forgot to mention, our blue-ribbon-winning homemade rolls are baked daily by my wife, also known as my first mate."

Without any more of his sales pitch, Rusty picked up his lobster kitchen tools. With years of practice, he was able to carefully extract large pieces of tail and claw meat from the five-pound steamed lobster that was on his cutting board.

Lloyd surmised that if his seafood was as good as his sales pitch, then he would certainly order something. Since Abby and Parker seemed to be already sold on his food, Lloyd asked, "Well, is anyone ready to order? I think I am!"

Rusty saw they were ready, so he took off his disposable nitro gloves and said, "So what excursion can I get for you today?"

Lloyd ordered the Captain Nemo, Abby asked for the Mermaid, and Parker said he would like to try the fried monkfish sandwich.

After the total cost of the lunches was paid, Rusty put on two new gloves to prepare their seafood. Within a few minutes, their food was ready. Rusty arranged the bowls and plates with silverware on a black-and-white checkered tray. Passing three trays out to them, he reached overhead and rang a loud brass ship's bell.

"Thank you, and eat hardy, my lads! Don't forget to tell everyone where you got your delicious meal. By the way, mates, I did not tell you before, but 10 percent of my profits go to our Port James food cupboard. No one, and I mean, *no one* in this world should be hungry."

Abby was so touched by his generosity, she reached into her pocketbook and gave him ten dollars for the food cupboard. She thanked him for his fundraiser and thought about how residents in Port James always seemed to pull together.

Parker helped with the tray, but just before taking it, he gave a salute to Rusty. Placed around the food truck area were picnic tables and benches where people could take their meals to eat. All three of them sat on the same side of the table so they could view the ocean. Someone had the foresight to put signs around that said stated *Please Do Not Feed the Seagulls.*

The carnival noise and general activity did not seem to bother the gulls, which were constantly circling in the sky. This afternoon, the ocean was relatively calm. Majestic cliffs that went on for hundreds of miles seemed to stand guard to protect the narrow sandy beaches. Lloyd said a quick prayer of thanks, both for their meal and the opportunity to share it with Abby and Parker. They then dug into their food.

In between morsels of lobster meat, Abby reached over and touched both Lloyd's and Parker's hands. Looking at her boys, she announced, "Goodness! That Rusty was right, this lunch of ours is fantastic! Besides all this, just smell that scrumptious sea salt air!"

Parker added to her observation and said in a loud, happy voice, "This is the best day of my life!"

After their meal, they found a barrel to put their recycles in and another table to return Rusty's checkered patterned tray. Parker was looking around where they were to decide what ride they should go on next. He had already eyed the huge Ferris wheel several times already. In fact, it was the first ride he noticed when they initially arrived.

"Mom and Dad, oh I mean, Lloyd, can we go on the Ferris wheel? Please? Pretty please?"

Abby had to assess whether she would venture on that monster ride but decided rather quickly. She knew she would never enjoy herself, but maybe Lloyd would go with her son. As they walked closer to the entrance, they noticed that there was no line at all. Most people were heading to either the food trucks or the entertainment stage where a local band was getting ready to play 1950s music.

The man operating the Ferris wheel saw them and quickly placed his glass soda bottle of Cherry Coke on the top of his control panel that was over the rotating gears. He waited there until it was time to help them on the ride. Abby sighed and looked at her men.

"Parker, are you sure you want to go on this this one? How about it, Lloyd, would you go with him? Now, my young man, let me zip up your jacket. You will probably be cold on that ride."

With that said, Abby turned Parker around and zipped his red jacket all the way to his little chin. While doing this motherly task, Lloyd said that he would take Parker even though he never liked heights.

To be sure, most of his projects included building roofs on gazebos and sheds, but this was so different. He never liked what seemed to be wires that were too weak for its purpose of holding it all together. Then too, besides going around and around, Ferris wheels always jiggled back and forth a lot. Lloyd's projects were always made of wood, and he made a practice of overbuilding each one. He used solid metal hangers to hold wood members together instead of toe-nailing. He also spent more money on his project by using pounds of hot-dipped galvanized wood screws instead of using nails.

So all in all, this ride would not be anything he would venture to go on. However, he looked at Abby and decided that he would offer to take him on the wheel.

Not noticed by either Abby or Lloyd, Parker ran up the Ferris wheel's entrance ramp and seated himself. The man lowered and locked the safety bar and started the rotation of the wheel. He then went a little out of sight to finish the rest of his soda from the bottle.

With a lump in their throat, all Abby and Lloyd could do was to remain on the ground, watching Parker going around and around with no one else on the entire wheel. Every time Parker went by them, he was smiling. With one hand, he gave a wave while keeping his other hand gripping the safety bar in front of him. Abby said, "Well, I guess that son of mine is growing up. Even though he ran up without you, he seems to be having fun. Here he comes again."

Then without any warning at all, the whole wheel stopped with a sudden and violent jerk. With terror in their eyes and within a split second, they saw Parker being shoved off his seat and going into a free fall to the ground.

CHAPTER 37

God's Will

Abby screamed at the top of her lungs as she helplessly watched her son. It seemed to be happening in slow motion and at lightning speed at the same time. She couldn't believe that God would allow this to happen.

As if God delivered a miracle to that place in Port James, and at that very split second, this terrible event took a turn. A fraction of a second after Parker's free fall, his hood twisted around and caught a protruding steel bolt from the side of the huge Ferris wheel. The zipper and his hood kept him hanging with his feet dangling helplessly but still alive. His little and helpless body was seventy or more feet from the ground.

Without thinking, if he could or could not bring himself to do what was needed, Lloyd jumped over the fence and mounted the Ferris wheel. Hand over hand, he inched up to his poor wiggling friend, the boy he loved with all his heart. Looking for his next hand-hold, he grabbed the next bolt. It was not in reach, so he used his toes to push from a cross brace to wrap his fingers around it.

He repeated this slow movement upward with a growing pain in his arms and hands. Lloyd was unaware that his fingers were being slashed by the sharp bolts until he felt the lifeblood trickling down into his armpits. His shirt became damp with his sweat and pulsating blood.

To reserve all his energy, Lloyd did not speak a word but prayed fervently in his mind to God.

"My God…please stay with me so I can find the next handhold. Please give me the strength I need."

After half of the way up, Lloyd found two crossbars where he could give his chest and leg muscles a needed rest.

Not wanting more than a fraction of a time to pass, he pushed on to the next rusty, sharp bolt. Within seconds, his body started to scream in unbelievable pain, asking him to give up.

By this time, other fairgoers started to run to the base of the Ferris wheel. Some were pointing up at Lloyd and Parker. Without exception, in their own personal and different ways, *they all were speaking whispered prayers* for his ability to reach the little boy.

From somewhere within the crowd, Beth bowed her head and prayed, "Oh God, Lloyd and little Parker came into my bakery a few days ago. They are so precious and have so much life to live. Please give them the opportunity to live!"

Pastor Wells quickly gathered his family close to him and prayed, "Heavenly Protector, You know what is happening before our eyes. Please deliver Your protection to precious little Parker and his buddy, Lloyd. We cannot possibly know how You can do this, but hear our desperate prayer. Please, please allow them to live! Amen."

At this moment, Lloyd felt his attempt was useless. He could not succeed in saving his friend or himself. His body was weakening after each second. He would have to let go and fall the sixty feet to the ground, most likely leaving Parker to die at the top of the wheel.

At that point of desperation, Parker stopped struggling and just hung quietly.

* * * * *

Then as the prayers were being received by God above, He delivered miraculous strength to Lloyd's muscles. Lloyd truly felt this added power surge through his muscles like a bolt of energy.

He knew it wasn't coming from anything he was doing. His body was still screaming and bleeding, but with God's given strength, he climbed swiftly and completely up to his little limp friend.

Releasing one hand that supported half his body weight, he swung his other hand over his head and grabbed the little red zippered jacket and the precious boy. Pushing both of his legs upward at the same instant and swinging in a powerful arch, Lloyd cascaded both of them onto the top chair.

CHAPTER 38

A Road Trip

The operator of the Ferris wheel kicked his broken glass bottle out of the gears that abruptly halted the ride. Within seconds, the Ferris wheel started to slowly bring its precious cargo safely back to the ground.

The operator stopped the motor, and Abby ran up to the seat where the boys laid. Showering them with tears, she checked for their injuries, then thanked God for delivering them back to her. Although shaking, she managed to get them off and placed them on some coats that bystanders had laid on the ground for them. Bloody and quivering, both boys gave her a small but totally priceless smile. The general manager of the carnival had been notified by Daisy, so he immediately called to have an ambulance waiting for them.

The emergency medical technicians placed them both on stretchers, with Abby walking at their side. Standing at the rear of the ambulance, the driver made sure the two stretchers were safely secured in the back. Looking over to Abby and just before closing the ambulance doors, he asked if she wanted to ride with them.

Without hesitation, Abby climbed inside and sat in between the boys. The one technician placed oxygen masks on both of her patients. The second technician started an intravenous to help Lloyd replace the fluid he had lost from his bleeding. Abby also noticed that finger clips to measure their pulses were recording their heartbeats.

After a few miles, the first responder sitting in the back slid open the window to the cab so he could talk to the driver.

"Frank, it's good news, looks like our patients are stable and are going to be just fine. Let's continue transporting them to emergency for a more complete medical assessment, just to be sure…and I don't think it is necessary to keep on the lights and siren."

Realization

The next morning, everyone at the Watercrests' had slept in a little later than normal. Jane prepared their little daybed for Parker to sleep next to Abby in her bedroom, just in case he needed help sometime throughout the night. Klem suggested that Lloyd should use the guest room for the same reason.

Eventually, everyone came down the stairs and made their way to settle around Jane's kitchen table. Jane greeted them and said, "I hope everyone doesn't expect a full breakfast this morning. As you can see, I have a selection of cereals on the table. In a second, I will get the milk from the refrigerator."

After a while, this family was feeling a little more normal. Thankfully. Klem waited for everyone to finish their cereal, then asked to say a blessing. Hands were folded, and heads bowed.

"Dear heavenly Protector. Yesterday, we all believe that You had delivered a miracle at the fairgrounds for our family. You gave Lloyd the necessary strength he needed. You sent medical people to make sure they were okay. In short, You sent them back to us in good health. For that and for all other blessings You give us daily, we offer our heartfelt thanks. Amen."

Then, little Parker added, "And thank You God for keeping that zipper on my jacket from letting me go! Amen."

He then turned to his mom and said, "Mom, I want to tell you something."

He looked at her for permission to continue. When she nodded, he weighed his little thoughts and words carefully and said, "When I was hanging there at the top of that ride, I saw something in the clouds. No, it wasn't in the clouds. It was kind of in front of me, sort of. But, Mom...it was real."

Now Parker had everyone's attention and were waiting for him to put together more of his thoughts. Abby gave a pat on his hand to let him know it was all right to continue.

"Well, like I said, it was real. I saw it, and I *felt* it too. In fact, the feeling was even stronger than actually seeing it. Mom...I was visited by one of God's angels."

"The angel said to me, 'Be at peace, child of God, you will not perish today. Your God has marvelous plans for you.' So, Mom, when I heard and felt this, I stopped struggling. I knew I did not have to struggle any longer."

Lloyd felt the goosebumps grow on the back of his head. He just had to share his story too.

"Well, family, halfway up to the climb that I had to make, I stalled. I had nothing left in me to continue. I then saw the same vision and *felt* that same angel. This angel from God's heaven gave me the strength to make it the rest of the way...right to you, Parker."

Out of respect for Parker and Lloyd, the room was completely silent, but even more so, for the awesomeness of their message and vision. After several minutes, Abby felt that she needed to share something else.

"Mom and Dad, since you were not there yesterday, you did not see what I saw. Parker and Lloyd, you didn't know it either. I am here to tell you that everyone at that fairground stopped what they were doing and gathered at the base of the Ferris wheel. Yes, they were in shock because of what was happening. But what I saw around me was incredible. *Everyone there were giving passionate prayers to God for Him to help and save you both. I mean everyone, even those I have no idea who they were.*

"I know there are good and wonderful people living in large and small cities, towns and villages. It is their own and unique place to live, *it is their home.* I have come to the appreciation and realization that *this is where I want to live for my home.*

"To be sure, I guess that I had to make that visit to New York City. I also believe that it was my obligation from the promise I made to Terri years ago. Now I truly feel deeply in my heart and soul that this little sea-swept Victorian village of Port James with every one of her precious residents are my people. And I love this place of wild cliffs, ocean surf, and also quiet beaches that God created with his own hands.

"My wonderful family, *I love you! I love you!* Mom and Dad, how could I ever, *ever* leave this life you have given me here in Port James?"

She extended her arms, and in unison, everyone did likewise. This little Port James family made a circle of hand-holding, sharing their love with each other.

Parker released his hands and used his napkin to absorb tears from his eyes. Placing his napkin back down on his little lap, he then looked around at his grandparents, his mom, and his buddy, Lloyd. With his innocent, child voice, he said, "Mom, I never, *ever* wanted to move from Port James. In fact, I had some bad nightmares when you were gone. But...Mom, what about that job in New York City?"

"Don't worry, Parker. Mr. Gram will find any number of other writers for his magazine. They are probably waiting in line for a chance to work there. Well, God bless them. *That was so not for me.* This truly has been and will always be my home, not New York City."

With total purity coming from a little boy, Parker then replied, "I bet people in that big city never smell the wonderful mix of the salty ocean air and freshly washed sheets blowing on the line in a backyard."

Klem and Jane gave a little smile but had a huge weight lifted off their souls. Their daughter and grandson were to continue living in this enchanting village of theirs. Maybe some more grandchildren would come along that they would be able to spoil with their love.

They felt so blessed having Abby's realization and final decision that they did not notice what Lloyd was up to.

Then, with Jane, Klem, and Parker looking on, Lloyd pulled out his chair and went on bended knee in front of Abby. With a gorgeous solitaire diamond engagement ring in his hand, he raised it up to her.

"My darling Abby, will you be my soul mate for life? Then after sharing our lives together on this earth, will you be my soul mate in heaven too?"

Abby's whole being was shaking from head to foot. To become Lloyd's wife was her overwhelming desire, but she did not expect this surprise today.

"Yes! Yes! Oh my goodness! Yes! *I will be yours forever!*"

Coming from the end of the footpath, there was the warm and familiar sound of the Port James lighthouse. It felt like an announcement of love.

Once again, contentment filled this little Port James home.

* * * * *

To all my readers from Abby

Dear friends,

I hope you do not mind if I can bend your ear for a few moments. I thank you in advance. As you know, after graduating from college, I became the source of much anxiety for my family. Yes, I put this on my parents, my son, and my best friend, Lloyd.

I think the turning point of my decision to stay in Port James started with Pastor Wells' sermon. He talked about being appreciative of everything around us, even a small, almost forgotten rose bush within the pageantry of other more majestic flowers.

It made me realize that *I should be appreciative of what I have*, friends, family, and a wonderful village to live in. Besides that, I also had my newfound love.

At the base of that Ferris wheel, the sincere way everyone prayed for Lloyd and Parker totally sealed my desire to forever stay and live in Port James. I want to personally thank everyone for all those passionate prayers. Each prayer meant so very much to me, more than I could ever express.

Besides these priceless gifts, every morning when I wake up, I thank God for my health and for another day to live.

A neighbor that my family has known for years has their father living with them. He cannot hear nor see too well, yet he has the best attitude, an attitude of appreciation for what he still has.

As you know, I wanted to relocate to explore the extent of my career in journalistic writing. You also know the outcome of that, but I definitely want to say something else.

This is what I will be telling my son Parker. If I am blessed with more children, I will also tell them, "If leaving your roots will help you blossom and grow by finding a fulfilling career, then that is the right path for you, and you should take it. Follow your dream. However, also please always carry these two ideals with you, no matter what path you take and no matter where you go.

First, *always remember who you are.* To get ahead, don't compromise the good principles and beliefs that we taught to you during your whole life. Never abandon those precious values. Stand true to what is good. Remember what God wants you to be and how He wants you to act every day of your life.

Second, *never forget where you have come from.* Remember your heritage...your hometown roots. If you must leave, carry these with you and be proud of where you have come from. Remember all the good things.

Finally, about the relationships, you must leave behind. Hold them close to you and cherish their love. They may have their faults, but always know, they love you. Like the old saying goes, 'Life is short.' It truly is.

No matter how well we try to plan each detail of our lives, we never know when our last day on earth will be. Relationships of friends and family are God's precious gift to us all; it is something to embrace and treasure. So always love them, and whenever you can, care for them."

Thank you for letting me tell you what I have learned firsthand. God bless you today and always.

Your friend,
Abby

EPILOGUE

Abby

After Lloyd finished the patio for the Lowells, they invited him to come back and visit with his fiancée. Dr. Doris Lowell offered Abby a position to help unify their many growing numbers of clinics. They needed a talented person with her background to organize and write a weekly newsletter. With overwhelming enthusiasm, Abby accepted the position. Soon, her work became invaluable, helping all the varied staff personnel to stay informed about each medical treatment center.

Terri

Abby recently received a letter from Terri. She is currently looking for work with another magazine in New York City.

Parker

Parker was officially adopted by Abby in time for him to be the proud ring bearer for their autumn wedding. He tells all his friends at school that one day, he is going to be a woodworker like Lloyd, his new official dad.

Lloyd

Lloyd enjoys surprising Abby with wonderful outings and, a few times a month, arranges adventures for Parker and him. His woodworking business in Port James is doing extremely well and is quite famous in the area.

The Watercrests

Klem and Jane celebrated their fiftieth wedding anniversary, including a reception the following summer, at the Port James lighthouse. They still make breakfasts together in their little kitchen and, by the grace of God, continue to truly enjoy their lives. After breakfast, Klem still walks up the short footpath to tend to his lighthouse and gift store.

God has blessed the residents of Port James, and life is good.

Afterword

Dear reader,

I hope you enjoyed this enchanting novel as much as I liked having these thoughts from sea-swept Port James, Maine, come to me. If you desire to experience more of these unforgettable and inspirational stories, I have listed the Port James Series for you.

Thank you for your love of reading and God's blessings to you and your family.

Sincerely,
Jay Diedreck

Klem Watercrest the Lighthouse Keeper
Seaside Journeys of Faith
A Port James Romance
I Hear My Lighthouse Calling

ABOUT THE AUTHOR

Jay and his wife, Alicia, enjoy village living in the northeast part of our country. They appreciate the beauty of all four seasons. Their summer vacations usually take them along the ocean coast, with a distinct desire to be in the State of Maine, where there are many lighthouses to explore.

After retirement, Jay began writing novels, this book being his fourth successful work.

Within a quiet place of their home, Jay sees his characters, and their actions appear like visions. He beautifully weaves them together, creating perfect and unforgettable experiences for his books.

It is a joy when readers express how they received powerful messages that once again give them balance and enjoyment in their lives.

Heartwarming, uplifting, and a story about the meaning of family, power of love, and doing what is right for everyone seems impossible, yet…the lighthouse is calling.

CPSIA information can be obtained
at www.ICGtesting.com
Printed in the USA
BVHW080433110921
616348BV00002B/13